THE GLASS FLOWERS

Cameron Stewart Miller

Chapter 1:
A Simple Game Of Tag

There is nothing worse than being cooped up inside against your will. Sure, Wake and Desi could have hopped out the front door and danced around in the rain, but it wasn't just the average Spring rainfall.

It was a torrential downpour.

All the boys could do was hope that the rain would let up before their weekend plans were ruined for good.

Wake plopped down onto his stomach next to Desi. "Stupid rain."

"We could put our rain gear on," Desi said, his eyes trained on the flickering TV screen. "It'll probably be pretty cold, though."

A flash of lightning outside caught Wake's eye. "I dunno." He cranked his head toward the gloomy hallway. "We could, but I don't think mom would be too happy if I took you out right now."

"Probably not."

They each sighed and focused back in on the colourful cartoons. It was one of Desi's favourite shows —one of those silly series anyone could watch where everything was back to its original place by the end of the episode. They watched as two cartoon boys worked together to humiliate their bully by pushing him into a pile of cow dung.

Gross.

Wake's attention was pulled back to the nearby window, and he watched a few raindrops streak down until they dripped out of view. He knew Desi was looking forward to playing out in the forest behind the house all week. Only now, They'd been thwarted by a bit of rain and aggressive thunder.

"Wake?" the boy's mother called from the stairs. "It looks like the weather's finally letting up. Why don't you take Desi out to play for a bit?"

"Okay, mom," Wake called back.

Desi gave Wake an excited look before sprinting into the hallway. They each rushed around the house grabbing their rain gear. The different moving boxes were in the way, but nothing was going to keep them from getting out of the house—not with one of their last chances to explore the forest staring right at them.

Desi's embarrassing galoshes—check.

Desi's oversized raincoat—check.

The young boy looked like a complete dork, but Wake knew exactly how it felt. They were old hand-me-downs after all.

The boys thumped toward the back door, and their mother leaned out of the kitchen as they traipsed through the living room. "It's going to be slippery so be careful. I don't want you taking him near that stream either, Wake. The rain might have—"

"Kay, mom," Wake said as he slid the door open for Desi. "We'll be back."

Wake stepped through and started sliding the door shut when he heard his mom again, "If it starts raining like that again—" The door slid into place and her voice sounded as if it were miles away.

It wasn't the first time they'd played in the forest after a rainstorm.

Wake and Desi were far apart in age, fourteen and seven respectively, but they were each rather responsible for their ages. They always got their homework done on time, and they could head outside without supervision, as long as Desi was attached to Wake's hip. They were mischievous like any other boys of their ages, but they earned their time to goof off.

The crisp, earthy air filled the boy's lungs as Desi splashed through the maze of puddles that was once an ordinary backyard. There was something so enchanting about the smell of the world after a storm. It was the kind of scent that the boys could have basked in for hours. That same air was cool, but the rain gear and promise of a fresh adventure made for zero complaints from the boys.

Wake swung the back gate open and stared into the heart of a dark green forest. "Alright, what game do you wanna play this time?"

"How about—" Desi jumped through the gate and splashed in a deep puddle, "—tag?" He stuck his tongue out before taking off toward the trees. "You're it first!"

"Hey! You little brat," Wake said as he took off after Desi.

The boys chased each other through the ancient forest. If they didn't know any better, it could have been mistaken for a jungle just by how vibrant and full of life it felt. The deeper they chased each other, the larger and larger the trees became.

They had traded a few tags—Wake had to slow himself down to avoid making his younger brother cry, so it was once again Wake's turn to chase Desi.

Desi looked back with a toothy grin. "Try to keep up with Super-Desi!"

Wake smirked and darted around a few trees. He knew exactly where they were, and exactly where Desi was headed. He rounded a small hill that dropped off to the ground below, and as Desi rushed past, Wake jumped down to meet him.

Wake landed right in front of Desi and tagged him hard. "You're it—Super-Desi."

"Aw, man."

"I already told you, you always take the same paths around here."

"It's easier," Desi shrugged.

"It is easier," Wake chuckled. "Easier for me to catch you." He shot off toward where he knew the stream his mother had warned him about was tucked away.

It was dangerous, sure, but it was always fun to chuck rocks into the rushing waters. Sometimes the boys would get lucky when the water was low and both sides of the stream would be filled with croaking frogs. One time they even spotted a deer as it stopped off for a quick drink.

Every single time they entered those woods they managed to see something new.

Wake had gotten quite a bit of distance from Desi as he arrived at the edge of the stream. "Mom wasn't kidding."

The stream had to be more than twice its normal size. They'd played in the stream before, but that was when it was at its usual level. The water being up to Wake's knees was one thing—the stream being able to swallow the boys up whole was an entirely different thing. The light drops of rain that had picked back up were only sure to add to the depth of the rushing water.

"Haha!" Desi shouted, far closer than Wake had assumed. "Gotcha!" He reached his hand out, but Wake instinctively dodged to the left.

Desi stumbled—right toward the stream.

He was going to fall in.

"Desi!" Wake wrapped a hand around his brother's arm, but the light sprinkling of rain had made his coat slippery. His hand flew off of Desi, and Wake watched as he tumbled into the dark stream.

After an eternal moment, Desi surfaced. "Wake!" He kicked and thrashed. "Help!"

Wake wasn't the best swimmer, but Desi couldn't swim at all. He could try to yell for someone to help, but it wasn't likely anyone would hear him. Wake could try to run back home, but there was no telling how long Desi could last in what had to be freezing cold water.

He had to go in.

"I—I'm coming, Desi," Wake said.

Wake stormed toward the stream and waded into the water. He was struggling to stay above the surface, and even Wake was finding that the water felt as if it was pulling him under into the cold depths. It was moments like those that made him wish he'd hurry up and hit a growth-spurt.

Wake wrapped an arm around Desi, but a sudden force pulled them both underwater. Everything became dark and confusing. The force of the water, the awful cold, the blinding panic—all of it making Wake unsure of what to do.

There was one thing he knew he could do.

Keep.

Swimming.

Forward.

He pulled Desi along until he reached the opposite side of the stream. Reaching out for anything to cling to, his hand met a root. He held it tight and pulled his way out of the stream with Desi still thrashing around.

They both shot up out of the water and tried to catch their breath. Wake could see that Desi was shaking as fiercely as he was. It felt like they had gone outside in the dead of winter in nothing but a couple of pairs of underwear.

"Desi," Wake patted his back. "You okay?"

The young boy nodded. It was almost impossible for Wake to see thanks to how soaked Desi was, but there were tears streaming down his cheeks.

"I think so." He wrapped his arms around Wake. "You saved me."

"What's family for?" Wake smiled and wrapped his arms around him. "Besides, If I headed back without you, I'm pretty sure mom would ground me for life."

Desi pulled away. "What the heck is that?"

Wake followed Desi's eyes up toward the top of the hill. Usually, the opposite side of the stream was just more of the same forest, but the sun had pierced through the clouds, and there was a bright shimmer oozing over the hill.

"I dunno," Wake said "But I'm gonna find out."

"Maybe we should just go home. Mom's gonna be mad we're soaked."

Wake took his coat off. "I can already feel the heat. We'll be dry in no time." He started toward the strange shimmer. "Come on."

Desi stayed on his heels as they reached the top of the hill. They stepped through the line of twisted trees and what they saw stopped them in their tracks.

"What? What are those?" Desi asked as he tossed his coat aside.

"I think—" Wake cocked his head. "I think they're flowers."

The boys had crossed the stream before.

They knew that there were more trees, more trails, and more rocks on this side.

That wasn't the case.

Not now.

"We've been here before," Desi squeezed Wake's arm. "This isn't supposed to be here."

"No. It's not."

Now, as far as the eye could see wasn't just more forest—stretching out across a series of hills were fields of odd shimmering flowers.

Wake spun around to where they had come from, but the stream was gone.

The entire forest was gone.

Everything they knew had disappeared.

In the place of the forest there was nothing but more fields of shimmering flowers.

Off in the distance, there sat a quiet village dotted with small huts the likes of which Wake had never seen before.

"Where are we?"

Chapter 2:
The Fields Of Glass Flowers

Wake crouched and stared at a row of dainty glass flowers. Up close, they were plain see-through glass, but at a distance, the flowers shimmered with different colours at different angles. Each and every one was as bizarre as the last.

He wrapped his fingers around the familiar earthy stem of an ordinary flower and picked it—the delicate glass petals all shining bright.

"This is unreal," Wake said.

"Have you ever seen something like this before?" Desi asked.

"What do you think?"

Rather than the weight of the glass ruining the stem, the glass seemed to be pulling up toward the sky. The flower twirled in his fingers and he watched as the petals danced in the light breeze. Wake stretched his arm up and let go of the flower.

It floated right up into the sky. The boys stared at it as it climbed higher and disappeared from sight.

Desi scratched his head. "How did you do that?"

"What?" Wake looked at his hands. "I didn't."

"What do you mean you didn't? Flowers can't fly. How else would it have floated away?"

He gestured toward the flowers. "You try if you don't believe me."

Desi gave him a funny look before crouching down and picking a flower of his own. He looked from Wake to the flower and then gave it a light toss into the air. The flower flew up a bit before settling in the air and slowly climbing up into the sky.

"See?" Wake said. "They're just—weird flowers."

Desi looked down at the flowers again. "I guess so." He kicked a group of them and more than a dozen danced through the air. "They are kinda cool, though."

Wake looked for anything resembling the forest they had come through, but the only trees in sight were dotted around the small village nearby. "I feel like I already know the answer to this, but have you ever come here before?"

"When am I out here without you?"

"That's what I thought." He brought a finger to his chin. "Any ideas on how to get back?"

"Uhm…" Desi shook his head. "No idea."

Wake pointed toward the village, taking note of the vast ocean sprawling out beyond it. "Maybe someone down there can help us. They must have a phone—or something."

"Those don't look like home."

Desi was right. The small huts had nothing on the sprawling homes in their neighbourhood. It was like they'd been transported to a whole new world the instant they made it across the stream.

Wake nudged Desi. "It's better than staying here and staring at weird flowers. I think—" The outline of a small figure ducking behind a bed of flowers caught Wake's eye. "Someone's watching us—or something is."

"What?" Desi asked in a panic. "Who?"

Wake nodded in the direction of the figure. Whatever or whoever it was, it was in between them and the village.

"Do you think it wants to hurt us?" Desi asked.

"No." Wake shook his head. "It's watching us. If it was going to hurt us, it probably would have already."

"You think?"

"Yep." He shot a hand into the air and waved at the figure. "Hey! Are these your flowers? We got kinda lost—can you maybe help us get back home?" Even from the long distance, the boys heard a slight shriek before the figure turned tail and barrelled toward the village. "Hey! Come back!"

"Great," Desi groaned. "You scared it off."

"Come on." Wake pulled him in the direction of the village. "Someone down there's gotta be able to help. They can't all be big scaredy-cats like you."

"I am not a scaredy-cat."

"You still like to sleep with a nightlight on."

"So?"

"So, that makes you a scaredy-cat."

"If that makes me a scaredy-cat, I don't want to be brave."

"Whatever, scaredy-cat."

The closer the boys got to the village, the more lively it felt. From the fields, they could only make out a single line of smoke floating up from the huts, but now, the sounds of laughter and conversation could be heard. That is until the boys reached the edge of the village, and everything fell silent. Even the smoke billowing out from the top of a larger hut had stopped altogether.

"Are you sure about this?" Desi clutched Wake's arm. "Something's wrong."

Desi was right, but Wake wasn't about to admit that out loud. The eerie quiet of the village gave it a kind of haunting quality. If the weather wasn't beautiful and sunny, even Wake might have been creeped out.

"Are you afraid a ghost is going to pop out and spook you?" Wake pulled his arm free and put on his best manly voice. "It's the middle of the day. Ghosts are scared of sunlight. The houses are weird, but I'm sure the people are nice."

Being so close to the wooden huts, they were a lot larger than they had originally looked. The largest hut of the village looked like it was only a bit smaller than their home.

"Where are all the people?" Desi looked around the quiet village. "That thing did run down here, right?"

"It did." Wake nodded as he stepped to the front door of the nearest structure. "Let's start knocking. There's gotta be a phone somewhere."

As he raised a fist, a barrel only a few steps away started to shake. The boys stared at it, not quite sure what to do. For whatever reason, Wake began to inch closer to it.

"What are you doing?" Desi asked in a hushed tone.

"I'm just going to take a peek."

"What if there's an angry animal in there or something?"

Wake wrapped his hands around the lid of the barrel. "When have we ever had problems with animals?"

"I don't like this."

Wake lifted the lid and took a step back, but nothing happened. The barrel had even stopped shaking. He nudged the barrel with his foot and they heard the same shriek they had heard from the figure in the fields of glass flowers.

He looked back at his nervous wreck of a brother, before shrugging and tipping the barrel onto it's side.

What looked like a small bear rolled out and looked up at the boys. "NO! PLEASE DON'T HURT ME!"

Wake's eyes nearly bugged out of his head. "It talked."

Desi had a similar look on his face. "It's—it's blue."

11

The blue creature examined each of the boys before getting to its feet and dusting itself off. "Of course I can talk, and of course I'm blue. What? You humans never seen a Kola before?"

The adorable creature's switch from a glass-shattering shriek to a gruff voice really threw the boys off.

As soon as the word *Kola* left its mouth, Wake knew what animal he was looking at. It wasn't a small bear, it looked exactly like a koala, only he had never seen one in real life. He couldn't help wondering if koalas were usually about waist-high, but he knew there was no such thing as a dark blue koala.

"You mean a koala?" Wake asked.

"Ko-a-la? What's a ko-a-la? I'm a Ko-la. Kola."

"A Kola. Okay…" Wake looked back at Desi for any hint of help, but Desi seemed just as astounded as he was. "Where is everyone? Is there anyone here that can help us figure out where we are? We were walking through the woods and then—"

"Then poof!" The Kola mimed an explosion. "You ended up in the field, right?"

Desi shot forward. "That's right. This has happened before?"

The Kola nodded. "If you know what's good for you, the two of you will leave and never come back."

"Why?"

"And how?" Wake added.

"Can't trust humans." The Kola's eyes darted around the village. "The last few—doesn't matter. Leave, now."

The door to the hut swung open. "What's all the fuss going on out—" A towering woman stepped out, and her eyes fell on the boys. "Oh! Hello there. Who are you?"

Wake felt himself turn pale as he stared at the woman. The woman wasn't a woman at all. Well—she was *half* a woman. The other half of her, the bottom half of her, was made up of the body and legs of an enormous spider. He knew if he was terrified, Desi must have been about ready to wet his pants.

The Kola held a hand up. "Don't worry, Ms. Ebbie, I've got this under control."

"Aza." Her eyes fell on the tipped barrel. "Were you hiding in my barrel again?"

"Maybe." Aza kicked some dirt. "There—there are humans. Real live humans, here—in our village. We need to get rid of them. You know what could happen if we—"

Ebbie cleared her throat and Aza froze. "What do we say, Aza?"

"There's a reason Aza isn't in charge."

"That's right."

"That's a talking spider." Desi nudged Wake. "A half-lady—half-spider. What is that thing?"

"I don't know." Wake brought a finger to his lips to quiet Desi.

Aza hopped in the air. "But the village is terrified!"

Ebbie sighed. "Is the village terrified by the humans, or did you terrify them on behalf of the humans without thinking things through?"

"The second part—I guess."

"That's what I thought." A warm smile spread across Ebbie's face as she turned her attention to the boys. "Now then, just who are you two? Quite rare we get human visitors around here."

Wake stepped toward Ebbie. "I'm—I'm Wake, ma'am. This—this is Desi. Where is *here*, exactly?"

Ebbie reached her hand out and rubbed Wake's face. "Poor things must be so frightened. You're both as pale as a glower on a cloudy day."

Wake looked at Desi, the poor kid's eyes were wider than an over-stuffed backpack. "Sorry. Desi has a bit of a fear of spiders."

Ebbie looked at her multitude of fuzzy legs before leaning toward him and running a hand through his hair. "I promise you have nothing to fear from me, child." Ebbie stood back up. "The two of you are standing in the centre of Mahlurma, one of the four travelling islands."

"Travelling islands?" Wake raised an eyebrow. "What does that mean?"

"See?" Aza scoffed. "They don't know anything. They won't make it a day here."

Ebbie scowled at Aza. "How can you expect them to know anything about a place they've never heard of?" Aza looked like it was afraid of Ebbie, but at the same time, it looked at her in the same way Wake did with his mother. She cleared her throat. "Everyone! Ignore Aza's warnings. There is no danger. These humans mean you no harm. Go about your business!"

In an instant, the quiet village turned into a bustling mess. Strange and colourful creatures with necks like giraffes peered from the windows of their huts. A small family of living mushrooms rushed through the dusty streets. A large happy bear waved at Ebbie before turning its attention to something that looked like a mustard-coloured alien.

Desi shook Wake's arm and pointed toward the village. "That thing—that's like Ebbie, but with tentacles for legs."

"Tentacles?" Ebbie looked toward where he had pointed and waved toward the creature. "Oh, that's just Olli. She's an absolute riot. Would you like me to introduce you?"

Desi leaned toward my ear. "Ask her how we can get home."

Ebbie had clearly heard Desi, but Wake cleared his throat anyway. "So, this is Mahlurma—how do we get back home? I've never heard of any Mahlurma. It's like we crossed that stream into a whole other world."

Ebbie nodded. "That's because you did." She stepped out into the road and held out her hands. "Come, I'd like to show you around the village. My husband should be back shortly—he knows better than I do when it comes to this sort of thing. We'll make you some supper and help you figure out how to get home. Okay?"

They watched Aza climb up Ebbie's legs until it was clung to her back like a backpack. Either Ebbie was weirdly strong, or that weird Kola was lighter than it looked. Wake stepped forward and placed a hand in hers and after a moment of collection, Desi did the same.

It felt strange for Wake to hold someone's hand like that. It had been years since he'd held his mother's hand while crossing the road, but it would be better to have someone who commanded so much respect on their side. If everyone reacted to Ebbie the same way Aza did, the boys were untouchable.

"O-okay." Desi was still shaking. "I t-t-trust you."

Ebbie replied with nothing but a gentle smile.

Wake looked up at Ebbie. "We're safe right? None of those things are gonna try to eat Desi?"

She shook her head. "As long as you remain by my side, no harm will come to either of you."

"Before we—uh—go, why are you guys afraid of humans? We aren't so bad."

"Why is Desi so afraid of spiders? We aren't so bad."

Desi looked worried all over again. "I got b-b-bit by a s-s-spider—and it really hurt."

"So you would judge all spiders because of the actions of one? That doesn't sound very fair to me."

Wake had never thought about things like that before. He'd seen plenty of spiders—some even crawled on him, without him ever being bit. What was the point of being afraid? Something bad could happen, sure, but something bad could happen at any time whether or not a spider was present.

"So some of the—" Wake narrowed his eyes. "Things here—judge humans because there've been some bad ones here?"

She smiled. "You're bright, young one." She started deeper into the bustling village, pulling the boys along. "Come, there's much to explain."

Chapter 3:
The Travelling Islands

The trip through the village was surprisingly nice. Aza ditched them for a stall full of food almost immediately, but the boys weren't about to complain about something like that. Some of the creatures wanted nothing to do with Desi and Wake, but most of them ended up coming around after some coaxing from Ebbie. It seemed like most of the creatures either looked up to or respected her in one way or another.

After a long walk, they came to an enormous cliff that dropped off into the raging sea below. Rather than bumpy rock walls, what Wake could see of the cliffs before they dove into the ocean below were smoother than a chalkboard. The smoothness was eerie and unnatural, something that gave the boys an uneasy feeling.

"The cliffs—" Wake trailed off.

Ebbie leaned closer to him. "What is it?"

"Usually cliffs are all bumpy and rocky, but these look smooth."

"That's because they are. Like a little slice cut out of a pie. The travelling islands need to be able to connect somehow."

Desi gave her a puzzled look. "So what does this island connect to?"

Ebbie pointed down at the cliffs. "This side connects to Cerulea." She stuck a thumb out in the opposite direction. "That side connects to Mulos." Finally, she pointed off to the side. "And over there is where Mahlurma connects to Voxal."

Wake looked out toward a wall of thick black smog in the direction of Voxal. Something about it seemed foreboding. The way the black smog seeped into the sky made the beautiful sight ugly and twisted as it shifted toward the island.

"And all those islands are constantly moving around?" Wake asked.

"Just about. The islands all move in their own unique patterns—all except for Voxal." Ebbie set her sight on the wall of smog. "That's the largest island—it remains stationary, only coming into contact with the other islands every six months. You'll want to steer clear of that one. Thankfully, our lovely island doesn't stick around there for too long. The smog would probably kill all of our crops if that were the case."

Wake had heard about Pangea, but the thought of a bunch of islands moving around and fitting together like puzzle pieces was insane. Ebbie had to be kidding around, but there wasn't a hint of a joke to be seen in her expression.

"So there's a bunch of islands—all moving around," Wake said. "That doesn't explain how we got here." He made a move to sit down on the ledge, but Ebbie pulled him back by the collar of his shirt. "Hey!"

She wagged a finger. "If you fall off that cliff, that's it for you. No one has ever been able to get back onto an island."

He stared down at the churning waters. "Good to know."

"I'm not sure how you humans end up in our lands,

but you aren't the first, and I'd guess that you won't be the last."

"Have any of them made it home?"

"It's hard to know. I have only met two other humans in my lifetime, but once they left our island, they never returned."

Wake could see an island coming into view over the horizon in the direction of where Ebbie said Cerulea was. There was no telling what that island was like, but if the boy's luck was going to continue, it was going to be just as strange.

"Do all the humans you see appear here?" Wake asked.

She shook her head. "I've heard tales of humans appearing on every island. The current head of Voxal—the human known as Conah—is said to have first appeared on the one island we don't connect with, Flurris."

Desi nudged his brother. "Mom is going to be so mad if we don't make it home in time for dinner."

"We've got a bit more to worry about than being late for dinner." Wake gave his brother a light punch in the arm. "We stepped out of our backyard and onto an island, Desi. We need to focus on getting home alive."

Wake could tell he had been a bit too harsh with him. The whole situation was just worrying, but it was worrying the both of them. It was hard to decide what to do next when every step had to involve protecting Desi.

"And you will." Ebbie wrapped her arms around the boys. "It may take a while, but we'll figure it out. Dub and I will do everything we can to help you, and you'll always be welcome on my island, okay?"

Desi hugged her back. "Thanks, Ebbie—but why are you being so nice to us?"

19

She brought a hand to her midsection. "I can't have children of my own, so it's nice to be able to play pretend, even if it's just for a little while."

Desi cocked his head. "Really?"

She folded her arms and winked. "Adults need to play pretend sometimes too."

"Ms. Ebbie!" Aza called as it did its best to run toward the trio. "Ms. Ebbie! I bumped into Dub on his way home. He sent me ahead to let you know he's coming over now." Aza reached them and placed its hands on its knees with a few good huffs of air. "Did I—do good?"

She smiled. "You did very good, Aza. Thank you."

"And how—are the—terrible two?"

Ebbie clicked her tongue. "Aza. That's enough of this. Wake and Desi are our guests—our friends, and you will treat them as such, right now. Is that understood?"

Aza glared at the boys. "Yes, Ms. Ebbie."

"Good."

Wake approached Aza and stuck out a hand. "I think we got off on the wrong—paw—"

"You think that's funny?" Aza asked.

"Aza." Ebbie warned.

Wake stifled a laugh. "No, I—I just—I'm sorry I tipped you out of the barrel. I wouldn't have done it if I knew you were—so friendly."

"Don't let it happen again." Aza studied him before putting a paw in his hand. "We can start over. Completely fresh. I'm Aza the Kola."

He shook Aza's paw. "I'm Wake."

"Wake." He looked over at Desi. "Desi, right? That short for something?"

Desi took a small step forward. "Desire."

Aza put its hand on its hips. "Mr. fancy-name over here."

"Dub-Dub!" Ebbie said with a big smile as she rushed toward a pig-like creature who'd been heading toward the group.

The creature wasn't just pig-like.

It was built just like any other normal human, but all of its features were that of a pig's. That, and it was almost twice the size of the average person.

Ebbie wrapped her entire spidery body around Dub as he spun her around. They looked as if they hadn't seen each other in years.

Dub set her down and looked at the boys. "What have we here? A new set of humans? I guess that explains why the village got so quiet. Been quite a while since we've had a visit from the likes of your kind."

Ebbie crawled toward them. "Dub, this is Wake and Desi. Boys, this is my wonderful husband Dub. He'll be able to explain to you boys just how to get home."

"Nice to meet you, sir," the boys said in unison.

"Sir?" Dub let out a squealing laugh. "Too formal for me. Dub will do." He pulled a small bag from behind him. "You boys like pie?"

They nodded, each praying a sweet treat was in their near future.

"Well then, let's head on home and have a slice. We can go over everything you need to do to get home once all our stomachs are full."

That morning, Wake and Desi were watching cartoons. Now, he and Desi were headed back to the house of a woman-spider and a walking, talking pig-man for a slice of pie, along with their loud-mouthed koala-thing.

Weirdest day ever.

Chapter 4:
The Keys to Getting Home

Neither Wake nor Desi had any idea what the home of a spider and pig would be like, but the simplicity of their hut still managed to surprise them both. In the centre of the room was a wooden table that they were all sat at. In one corner were some linens that Wake assumed they used for makeshift beds. Another corner was complete with a fireplace and the other two simply housed various supplies and cabinets.

Nice and simple. It almost felt like home.

"Pie-pie-pie—how I love some pie—pie-pie-pie—I love-a-dah pie!" Dub sang as he sat at the table.

"Good apples too." The entirety of the hut had filled with the scent of fresh apple pie as Ebbie cut everyone a slice. "Must have been just awful to make."

"Awful?" Wake looked over at the pie. "Why awful?"

Ebbie and Dub shared a look. "It's a long story."

Ebbie set the pieces of pie down in front of everyone, but Desi curled a lip at his. "No offence, but there isn't anything weird in this, is there? Just apples and crust?"

Dub nodded. "Simple recipe. Nothing fancy. Apples, sugar, lots of butter."

Wake took a bite of what had to be the best pie he'd ever tasted. It almost seemed rude to his mom that he preferred this pie over anything she'd ever made.

Somehow these monstrous creatures were terrific bakers. That old idea of not judging a book by its cover was really making a lot of sense.

Wake let out an involuntary hum. "This is so good."

Desi took a bite of his slice and did the same. "This is better than mom's."

"I was thinking the same thing."

Desi poked Wake and gestured to Dub who was gorging himself on his large slice of pie. "Looks like we aren't the only ones who like it."

Ebbie giggled. "Excuse him. Apple pie is his absolute favourite."

Dub licked his plate clean and set it down. "What? Can a happy hog not enjoy a delicious piece of pie anymore?" He leaned back in his chair and stretched. "You lads wanted to learn how to get home, right?"

Desi nodded. "Yes, sir—uh—Dub."

Dub leaned forward. "I'm going to be honest with you boys because Ebbie seems to have taken a liking to you—it's not going to be easy."

Ebbie put a hand on his. "But, they can do it." She turned her attention to the boys. "Just because something isn't going to be easy doesn't mean it will be impossible."

"Right." He nodded. "You lads seem bright. You'll be okay."

Wake and Desi shared a look. "So, what do we have to do?"

"You'll need to find yourselves five artifacts." Dub grabbed a handful of napkins and laid five out on the table. "One from each of the five islands. Once you've managed to grab all five, you just need to return to where you first came into this world, and you should be able to return to your home—at least, that's what they say."

"What kind of artifacts?" Desi asked. "What do they look like?"

Aza nibbled on its piece of the pie. "I bet they're shiny."

Dub rubbed his chin. "What do they look like? Well, they—they kind of—I guess you could say—" Dub turned to Ebbie. "Could you be a dear and douse the fireplace? I need a piece of charcoal."

She nodded and grabbed a small bowl of water. After a quick moment, she came back with a piece of charcoal and handed it to Dub. "Here, love."

"Thank you, my dear." Dub started drawing on the napkins. "The Cerulea artifact is this strange key. It's held by a powerful wizard." He set the napkin aside and got to work on the next one.

"Wait, like a real wizard?" Desi wiggled his fingers. "With magic?"

Dub nodded. "The Flurris artifact is this strange orb. It's the prized possession of the Hog King."

"Wizards *and* Hog Kings?" Wake asked. "You guys related?"

"Thankfully, no."

Dub got to work on the third drawing. "The Mulos artifact is a strange pot. I don't know much about it other than that." He set the drawing aside and sighed at a blank napkin. "The Voxal Artifact is completely unknown, aside from the fact that it is kept close by Conah. Find him, you'll find the artifact."

"And what about the Mahlurma artifact?" Wake asked.

Dub pulled a small glowing sack from his pocket. "That would be this bag of seeds."

Desi grinned. "This is great! We already have one!"

"One down. Four to go," Wake said as he high-fived Desi.

Dub cleared his throat and put the sack away. "I can't just give this to you. Not yet."

"Why not?"

"You'll find that getting each of the artifacts is not as simple as simply asking someone to hand them over. It's going to be a long and difficult journey."

Wake fiddled with his fork. "Okay, so what do we have to do?"

Dub looked out the window toward the setting sun. "You boys can spend the night here. We'll get up first thing in the morning and I'll show you exactly what I need done before I can give you these seeds. Does that sound alright?"

Wake looked at the sunset. "We really should get going as soon as possible. Our mom—"

"Would be worried if her two boys were running around unsupervised in the middle of the night—in a strange land," Ebbie said. "Travelling in the dark isn't going to do you any good. Besides, you can't move on until tomorrow afternoon anyway, that's when Mahlurma and Cerulea will connect."

Desi pushed his plate forward. "How does all of that work? How long do the islands stay connected?"

"You'll have one hour to cross to the new island once they're connected," Ebbie said as she grabbed everyone's plates. "It takes a day for the islands to meet each other. Miss the hour to cross and you'll be stuck for quite a while."

Dub cleared his throat. "It's different for Voxal, though. Everyone gets two hours to do their business on Voxal before the islands pull back for six months. You get stuck there, it'll be a long time before you'll get a chance to leave again. Pay attention to when the islands start approaching that smoggy hole."

"This is a lot of information." Wake put a hand on his head. "It feels like my head is gonna burst."

"It is a lot," Dub smiled. "But I have a feeling the two of you will be just fine."

"I'll lay out some places for you boys." Ebbie grabbed a bunch of sheets. "You'll be safe here tonight, and we'll say our goodbyes tomorrow when Cerulea and Mahlurma merge, okay?"

Wake nodded. "Should we find some weapons or something?"

Dub chuckled. "Violent little humans."

Ebbie shook her head. "Not the best idea. You'll probably have your fair share of problems just being human." She put a hand on Aza. "You can take Aza with you tomorrow. He'll help guide you and keep you safe."

"What?" Aza asked. "Are you sure?"

"You do owe us a favour."

It groaned. "Fine. I'll keep the kids safe. Tomorrow only."

She smiled. "Thank you, Aza."

"You're welcome Ms. Ebbie."

Wake flicked Desi's hand. "You okay?"

"I think so," he said. "I'm just a bit worried."

"We'll find our way home and explain everything to mom. It's not like we're going to get into any trouble, she'll just be happy to have us back. She's probably already freaking out."

Ebbie nodded. "I know I would be. That's why we're doing what we can to help." She gave the boys a light squeeze on the shoulder. "Now then, let's all get some shut-eye."

Chapter 5:
Fresh Fruit With Faces

For a pig, Dub sure wasn't lazy.

As soon as the sun peeked over the horizon he hauled Desi and Wake out of bed. Whatever it was that he wanted them to do, Wake wished it could have waited another hour or two. Sleeping could already be hard enough, but if you throw in a hut full of creatures while you're sleeping, it can become even harder.

As they rounded the back of the hut they were faced with a small enclosure. It was the standard farmers' field for cattle to roam around in, with one slight change. Rather than cows or sheep, the field was filled with what looked to be large fish, all thumping around on strange sets of legs.

Wake pointed at one of the creatures. "Are those fish —cows—fish-cows?"

Dub scratched his belly. "Cow? What's a cow"

"It's like a—well, it's sort of—"

"Like those things," Desi said. "But with black and white spots."

Dub stared at the boys like he didn't believe them. "Creatures with black and white spots?" He laughed so hard his belly shook. "These here are aquavine. Spots— you humans sure do come from a strange land, don't you?"

"Sure," Desi looked over at Wake as Dub made his way into the enclosure. "We're the ones that come from a strange place."

They followed close behind Dub and watched as one of the creatures jumped multiple stories into the air. It didn't look like it took the creature much effort at all.

Desi stared up at it. "Is that thing going to smash into the ground?"

"Yeah," Dub looked up as the aquavine started a speedy descent. "They tend to land on their feet."

The creature landed on the ground with a dull look on its face. It had gone higher than any rollercoaster either of the boys had ever been on, so the calm look was surprising. Wake let out a small chuckle at the lack of a reaction on the creature's face.

"Wait a second." Wake clued into a fact he hoped wasn't true. "You aren't going to make us ride these things are you?"

Dub snorted. "Well, of course." He slapped his thighs and one of the aquavine lumbered over. "They're the quickest way to travel around the island here."

"I'm not so good with heights," Desi said.

"This here is Saran." Dub ran his hand along the aquavine's body. "She's a good girl." He grabbed a large saddle and placed it on the creature's back. "The both of you will be able to ride her. She doesn't jump for height, she jumps for distance, so you won't go quite as high as some of the others here jump."

Wake inched closer to Saran and ran a hand along her scaly back. "You want us to just ride her around? That's it? Then we can have those seeds?"

"Not quite." Dub lifted Wake onto Saran. "The old girl knows where she's headed, and how to get home." He lifted Desi up onto Saran as well. "She's going to take you across the island to a big farm." He pulled two small satchels from a bag of his own and handed them to the boys. "Pick us lots of fruit—whatever you'd like, and then come on back."

Desi inspected his satchel. "That doesn't sound too bad."

Aza came around the corner of the hut and made its way over with a stretch. "It's too early for this."

"You're late." Dub snatched Aza and tossed it up behind Desi. He wiggled a finger at Desi "And it doesn't sound too bad because I didn't get to the bad part yet."

Desi gulped. "Oh."

Dub laughed his way into a snorting fit. "You're small boys, you'll be fine. You just need to avoid the farmer, because he doesn't like it when strangers are messing with his crops."

"Avoid the farmer?" Wake gripped the saddle. "Why don't you just go?"

Dub scratched his belly. "The village hasn't been welcome since some of the villagers took a little more than they should have from the farm. We've been sneaking fruits and vegetables in secret the past little while."

Desi started to shake. "B-but w-what happens if the farmer catches us?"

Dub sighed. "Don't get caught. Aza can help fill you in."

Aza groaned. "Of course I can."

Dub crouched near Saran's face. "As long as you get some fruit, you just hop right back on Saran and you'll be fine, got it?" The boys nodded and Dub smiled. "Well then, go on and get!" Dub tickled Saran's back legs and she launched away from the village.

"WHOA!" the boys shrieked.

Wake held the saddle for dear life, and Desi did the same to Wake. The rushing air was freeing, and being able to see the beauty of Mahlurma from above was a treat. It reminded Wake of a few years ago when he got to go on vacation with his parents. It was a beautiful tropical island.

"ARE WE ALMOST THERE?" Desi shouted in Wake's ear.

"You don't need to yell," Wake replied.

"SORRY—sorry."

Wake scanned the distance each time Saran hit the peak of her jump. He spotted an enormous farm off in the distance. "There. I think that's it."

"Are you sure?"

Wake shrugged. "It's the only thing I've seen since we left the village and we're headed right for it, so, yeah. I'm sure."

"You got it!" Aza called.

At the top of another jump, Wake spotted a few different farm buildings near some cliffs. There were what had to be hundreds of miles of crops in one section, and rows of enormous trees in another.

"How much longer do you think it'll take?" Desi asked.

They landed in the middle of a strange forest filled with beetles that were the size of minivans before Saran leaped again.

"Probably a while," Wake said plainly. "We're moving pretty fast, but it's really far—"

"DID YOU SEE THOSE THINGS?"

"Yelling," Wake warned. "Yes, Desi. I saw them. Everything here is weird."

"Those were bugs! They were huge. Bugs are supposed to be little—so you can step on them."

"I know!" Wake rolled his eyes. "I saw!"

"I'm sorry."

There was a bit of an awkward pause in the air.

Wake sighed. "I think we'll be there in ten—fifteen minutes tops." Of course, Wake had no idea how long it would take. He just wanted to get Desi to relax a bit and shut up. He could feel Desi's nerves radiating toward him, and his yelling was only irritating Wake even more. "Right, Aza?"

"More or less."

Desi tightened his grip. "Oh, great."

"Just close your eyes," Aza said as he itched himself "We'll be there in no time."

"Way ahead of you on that."

After a few more leaps and a few more minutes, Saran came to a complete halt at a small fence. They were right on the edge of the farm where the crops met the massive trees. Everything was quiet, but a tinge of worry tugged at Wake. What if the farmer had seen their approach?

"Looks like we're here." Wake climbed off of Saran and ran his hand along her head. "Good job—girl."

Desi hopped down and scratched underneath Saran's head. "You did good. Maybe on our way back, let's not jump quite so high?"

Saran replied with a dull look.

"You ready?" Wake stared off toward the crops. "Let's grab what we can quick. Maybe we won't even need to worry about this farmer—" Wake looked over at Aza as the Kola lounged on Saran. "You coming?"

"You boys go ahead." It waved a paw. "I doubt you'll even see the farmer. If you hear any loud thumps, hide behind something."

"You need to help too."

"It's just fruit. I don't even have a bag anyway. Think of me more as a guide than a helpful grunt."

Wake sighed. "Thanks, Aza."

Desi tapped his brother. "What should we grab?"

"Anything, I guess." The boys hopped the fence and started toward the vegetation. "As long as the bags are full, we should be good to go."

Desi pointed toward the nearest tree. "Looks like there are some apples we can pick."

Wake looked from the nearby trees to the ones deeper in the farm. The trees by the boys were about the same size as usual, but as the trees continued along, the larger and larger they became. It even looked like the big trees had even bigger pieces of fruit hanging from their branches.

"I didn't think any of this fruit could grow in the same place. Maybe the farmers back home are just lazy or something." Wake looked from the tree to some nearby vines of grapes. "I'll try to climb the tree. You go get some of those grapes"

Desi nabbed a fallen apple from the grass. "What if we just grabbed what's already on the ground?"

Wake shrugged. "Mom always said you can't pick the apples from the ground, remember?"

"But it looks fine to me."

"Look," Wake snatched the apple from his brother and threw it in his bag. "If that farmer ends up coming around, we'll grab what we can from the ground." He shuffled toward the tree. "Let's try to get what we can fresh from the trees. It's not nice to make Ebbie and Dub eat food from the ground."

Desi nodded and headed toward the vines as Wake approached the apple tree. Luckily, climbing trees was one of Wake's favourite forest pastimes—when they weren't soaking wet from the rain. If the boys played hide and seek in the woods, he'd often climb up a tree because Desi wouldn't even think to look up.

The tree looked like any other apple tree he'd seen before, but it felt—different. The rough bark felt more like a kind of foam in his hands as he shimmied up the tree. It was much nicer than climbing trees back home since the soft foam-like texture kept him from getting covered in scratches on his way up.

He stopped on a sturdy branch and looked down to Desi as the boy plucked grapes and tossed them into his bag. "I guess this beats math class."

Wake reached for a nearby apple, but a slight rumbling in his satchel caught his attention.

"Where am I? It's so dark in here." a muffled voice said.

He stared down at his satchel. Whatever had just spoken, was definitely inside the bag. After the whole mess with Aza the day before, Wake's mind wandered to just what it could be.

Some kind of talking bug?

A tiny creature that clung to that apple without either of the boys knowing it had?

Aza's weird cousin?

Wake flipped open the bag and looked down at the apple he had tossed in. "What in the—"

Two eyes, clearly belonging to the apple, popped open and blinked a few times.

If the bag wasn't attached to Wake, he would have sent it flying.

"Hey! Did you put me in here?" the apple asked.

"You're an apple," Wake said.

"I am."

"And you're talking."

"I am." Somehow, the apple actually looked confused. "You're a human and you're talking. What's the big deal?"

"What is going on?" Wake muttered to himself.

"I'm wondering the same thing. First, I fall out of the tree, and then after a small nap I wake up in total darkness."

"If you're alive, does that mean—" Wake got his answer when he heard Desi shriek. "The grapes are too, aren't they?"

"Yup!" the apple replied. "Welcome to The Living Farm."

Wake sat down on the branch. "What's your name?"

"You can call me Mac."

"Alright, Mac. Are you going to be upset if I pick some of your—friends?"

Mac gasped. "Is it so you can make a pie? Please tell me it's so you can make a pie. It's every apple's dream to become a pie."

"But doesn't that mean you'd—"

"Yes, yes, but if you feed the planet, the planet feeds you," Mac said with a satisfied grin. "The beings here take great care of us—feed us—protect us. It's only fair that we pay that back how we can."

Wake frowned. "That's kind of sad."

"That's not sad. That's life. Everything—all life— works in tandem to see that life—this world—can continue to thrive."

"Are all you fruit so—wordy?"

"No." Mac laughed. "The others tell me to shut it all the time. You should hear me get into philosophy—"

THUMP!

THUMP!

THUMP!

"You're going to want to hide," Mac winced.

The thumps sounded like explosions were going off, and they were only getting closer and closer. The shaking of the tree nearly threw Wake to the fruit-littered ground below. He caught himself and leaned against the trunk.

The enormous buildings.

The gigantic trees.

The thunderous steps.

It all made sense.

THUMP!
THUMP!
THUMP!

The farmer had to be some kind of giant.

A giant what?

That was the real question.

Wake looked down at Desi as the thumping grew closer. Even from a distance, he could see Desi was shaking like a frightened chihuahua. He had gotten as flat as he could with his back to a small mound of dirt. It wasn't much, but it would keep him hidden.

"Mac," Wake whispered as he pulled him out of the bag. "What the heck is that?"

"The farmer," Mac whispered back. "He doesn't like visitors."

Wake peered around the tree and the gigantic form of the monstrous farmer came into view. It was a strange creature, one without a body. It was an enormous head with long thin arms and legs—and it did *not* look happy.

"I could have sworn I spotted one of those aquavine headed this way again," the farmer growled.

Wake looked down at Desi again, but this time it looked like he was crying. "Mac? If I throw you down to my brother, can you keep him calm?"

"Throw me? Oh, oh, oh." He winced at the ground. "Just—just aim for some soft dirt, okay?"

Wake nodded and chucked Mac down to Desi. It was a great throw, but Desi was so jumpy that the impact caused him to gasp. It was so loud Wake could hear it, so he wondered what that could mean for a giant's hearing.

"Hmm?" The farmer thumped closer. "Is there someone there?" It got down on its hands and knees, only a few feet away from where Desi was hidden. "If you're from the village, just come out. If not, when I find you, I'll eat you!"

Wake needed to think fast. The farmer was closing in on where Desi was hidden, but what could either of them do? It's not like they could fight the farmer—they'd be lucky if they could even get away from him.

Wake couldn't help but feel relieved when he saw Aza walking toward the farmer.

"Singo!" Aza called as it strutted toward the farmer. "Long time no see!"

"Aza? That aquavine was you? What are you doing here?"

"It was indeed!" Aza's eyes flicked toward Wake and then back to Singo. "I'm here to negotiate on behalf of the village. We'd like to get some more fruit."

"You?" Singo let out a hearty laugh. "They sent dimwitted little Aza here to speak with me?"

"Watch it." Aza crossed its arms. "Let's go have a chat in your home." Aza's tone shifted as it flicked its eyes from Desi to Wake. "I'll only need five minutes."

Singo stood back up and brought a finger to his chin. "I don't know what you're up to, but I'll hear you out. Come."

"Right away, sir." Aza looked up at Wake. "My aquavine better still be waiting for me when I get back."

"Why wouldn't it be?" Singo asked.

Asa's attention snapped back to the farmer. "No reason."

Once Aza and Singo were far enough away, Wake plucked a couple of apples and tossed them in his bag. They weren't talking, so he figured they must have been napping as Mac had mentioned.

It didn't look like Desi had moved much so Wake scrambled out of the tree and over to him. "Desi, you okay?"

"Hello, again!" Mac said with a smile.

"Hi, Mac."

"Why?" Desi was still shaking as he stared at Mac. "Why is all the fruit talking?"

"Weird place full of weird things." Wake helped him to his feet. "You get some grapes?"

He nodded. "Filled half my pack."

Wake looked past the grapes at rows of different coloured berries. "Let's make this easy and fill the rest of our bags with those. Like Aza said, five minutes."

Desi picked up Mac. "Thanks for trying to help me."

"No problem, Desi. What are friends for?"

"We're friends?"

"I'd sure say so!" Mac said with a smile.

It took no time at all to fill the rest of the satchels with the different berries. Though it was strange to pick berries that talked back. Each time Wake grabbed a berry they'd speak.

"Hi!" a raspberry said.

"Hello," Wake said in an awkward tone. "Sorry."

PICK!

"Hi there!" a blueberry said.

"Hello. Sorry."

YOINK!

"How's it going?" a gooseberry asked.

"It's going."

SNAG!

After a few minutes, Desi tapped Wake and pointed toward where the farmer had left. "I think time's up. What do we do?"

Wake flipped his pack shut. "Back to Saran. We just gotta wait for—"

"RUN!" Aza screeched as it sprinted toward the boys.

Chapter 6:
A BIG Chase

"What happened?" Wake asked as Aza sprinted toward them.

"Negotiations broke down!" Aza said.

"What does that mean?"

"Get back to Saran!"

THUMP!
THUMP!
THUMP!

The boys rushed back toward their aquavine with Aza right on their heels. All the while the thumping of the gigantic farmer grew closer and closer. Just a bit further and they'd be off of the farm. One step closer to getting home.

"Are we going to make it?" Desi asked.

"Just keep running," Wake said.

A hand slapped down just behind them, sending them all sprawling in different directions.

"You two, hide! It's every Kola for himself!" Aza shouted, before diving behind a nearby tree.

Wake grabbed the back of Desi's shirt before he was even back to his feet and tossed him as hard as he could. "I'll distract him. Get Aza and get back to Saran. I'll meet you there."

Desi tumbled right behind a large tree as Wake ran further into the field to find a tree of his own to hide behind.

"Where do you think you're going, human?" Singo's voice boomed as he thumped toward him.

"At least he's coming for me," Wake said to himself as he weaved in and out of the trees.

Luckily, Singo wasn't interested in destroying his crops and trees to catch a couple of trespassers, so Wake managed to put some distance between them. After he couldn't see Singo anymore, he hid behind a huge tree to catch his breath.

"WHERE DID YOU GO?!" the farmer sounded like he was right on the other side of the tree, but Wake wasn't about to stick his head out to see if that was true.

"Psssst," a voice whispered. "Hey! Down here!"

Wake looked down to see a happy pear smiling up at him. "Now's—really not—the time."

"You must be what's got Singo all riled up, huh?" the pear asked.

"You could say that."

"Need some help?"

"No offence," Wake raised an eyebrow. "But how do you—a little pear—think you're going to help me escape a giant?"

"First of all, you can call me Perry. Perry the pear."

"Of course that's your name."

"Second of all, just gimme a toss."

"GRAH! COME OUT NOW!" Singo shouted.

Wake paused for a second, and then snatched Perry from the ground. "Where am I throwing you and how is it supposed to help?"

"Throw me as high and as far as you can. I promise I'll distract him."

"I'm throwing a lot of talking fruit today." Wake sighed. "Why would you even help me?"

Perry's eyes darted around. "What else am I gonna do today?"

"Good point. You ready?"

Perry narrowed his eyes. "Let's do it."

The small pear took a deep breath in and Wake chucked him as hard as he could. After he had passed a couple of trees, Perry let out the loudest scream possible —way louder than Wake thought a piece of fruit could have screamed. Something which was a weird thought in itself.

How could a fruit talk, let alone scream?

"I HEAR YOU!" Singo shouted as he started after Perry.

THUMP!
THUMP!
THUMP!

The answer to the question of how fruit could talk didn't matter, because Perry's idea had worked. It would have been weird if someone like Ebbie or Dub saved Wake's life, but a pear was a different kind of weird.

Wake doubled back to where he had left Desi, but he was gone.

He spun around. "Desi?"

Desi's head popped out from behind the smallest tree at the edge of the farm. "Wake? What was that scream?"

"A helpful pear named Perry."

"A pear named Perry?"

"A pear named Perry." Wake looked around. "Where's Aza?"

"Right here," Aza said as it hopped out of a tree to Wake's left. "Smart thinking, getting the fruit to help."

"TRICKS!" Singo's screams echoed across the farm. He turned and set his sights on the group once again as he tossed Perry into his gigantic mouth. "AZA! YOU'LL

BE WORKING ON MY FARM FOR YEARS FOR THIS!"

"Not smart enough," Wake said.

Aza shrugged. "Got us enough distance to get out of here."

"You sure?"

"Nope. Time to run."

They rushed toward the fence again, all the while Singo's stomps almost caused their legs to buckle with each massive step.

THUMP!
THUMP!
THUMP!

"Over the fence?" Desi asked.

"Over the fence!" Aza replied.

They hopped the fence to Saran and Aza turned her around. "You gotta jump as far as you can, girl."

"GET BACK HERE, AZA!"

"No thank you!"

They all climbed onto Saran and took a look back. Singo was reaching out to grab all of them. All it would have taken was one quick movement to squish them all.

Aza tickled the sides of Saran and she shot into the air in the direction of the village. Singo screamed and threw a tantrum as they hopped away. Luckily the journey back to the village would have been a long one, even for a giant as strange as Singo.

Wake tried to catch his breath. "That's enough — excitement—for one day."

He ran his hand along Saran's side and she gave Wake a happy look. She must have been used to hopping such huge distances because if Wake were her, he'd keep his eyes forward at all times. There were a lot of things that could go wrong while you're flying through the air.

"It can't get much harder than that, can it?" Desi asked.

Wake brought a hand to his face. "Why do you always have to do that?"

"What?"

"If it wasn't going to be harder before, it definitely is after you said something like that," Wake said.

"How does that make any sense?"

"It's just the way the world works."

Aza nodded in agreement. "Wake's not wrong."

"Do you think we got enough fruit?" Wake flipped his pack open for Aza.

"More than enough." Aza flipped it shut again. "If I were in charge of the artifact, I'd let you kids have it."

Wake decided against looking back at the farm one last time. Looking back wasn't going to help him and Desi find a way home. Instead, he looked forward to Aza's village. For the first stop on their crazy adventure, things could have gone worse.

Chapter 7:
Off To See Amphinara

By the time the trio arrived back to the Ebbie's village, Cerulea was close enough to reach out and grab Mahlurma. Ebbie and Dub must have spotted them boys hopping their way back because they were already waiting to greet them.

When Saran came to a stop, both the boys fell to the ground and kissed it. It was much nicer to be back on solid ground, even if the ride was kind of fun. Still, that was more hopping than either of the boys ever needed in their lives.

Dub narrowed his eyes. "You boys make out okay?"

They each revealed their bags filled with fruit, and Ebbie clasped her hands. "Oh, I knew you'd do wonderfully, and here you are. Look at all that!"

Wake scratched the back of his neck. "There's some apples and grapes under all the berries. Lot's of blueberries, blackberries, raspberries, and gooseberries."

"Hi there," all the fruit said in unison.

"You forgot to mention that the fruit talked," Wake said as he and Desi handed their bags to Dub.

Dub grabbed a nearby bucket and emptied all the fruit into it.

"Weeeeeeee!" the fruit said as they tumbled.

"Sorry." Dub snorted. "It's something you get used to. I guess that's not the norm for humans?"

Desi scoffed. "Nothing here is the norm for us."

Dub handed the satchels back to the boy. "You two can keep these for your journey. You'll make better use of them than we will."

"Are you sure?"

Dub nodded. "It'll help you carry all those artifacts —oh!" He pulled the drawings he'd made of the artifacts from his pocket and shoved them into Wake's bag. "Can't forget these. Just in case."

"And these meals I made for you boys," Ebbie said as she put little wraps into the bags.

The boys lit up. "Thanks, Ebbie."

She patted their heads. "Don't eat them too quick. They'll last you a little while, but you'll have to find some more food for yourselves at some point."

"So." Wake looked at Dub.

"So?" Dub gave a confused look in return.

"The seeds?"

"Oh! Right!" He pulled out the bag of seeds. "We wanted to talk to you boys about that before we walked you over to Cerulea."

"Talk about what?"

"We thought we could hold onto them for you."

"What? But we did what you wanted," Desi said in a panic. "We got you the fruit."

Dub waved his hands. "Calm down, lad. I just mean, you'll be going on a long adventure, and you have to come back here to get home anyway. If we hold onto them until you get back, you won't have to worry about losing them."

"Oh, I get it."

Wake nodded. "That's a good idea."

Ebbie put a hand on his shoulder. "Besides, if we hang onto them, then you boys have to come and say goodbye before you go."

Wake smiled. "We wouldn't leave without saying

bye."

"Of course," Dub placed the bucket of fruit on their window sill. "The good ones all know the importance of goodbyes. You two did great, so we'll say that we owe you our artifact. Alright?" The boys nodded. "Aza, were you much of a pain for the boys?"

Aza rolled its eyes. "I'll have you know that I—"

"Aza saved us," Desi said. "That weird farmer was about to find us, but it distracted that thing for us."

"That so?" Dub asked as he opened the gate for Saran to join her aquavine heard.

Watching the large creature lumber into the enclosure was strange. It was so fast and powerful when it wanted to be, but it looked like all it wanted to do was nap.

"You bet it's so."

"Well, then I suppose Ebbie will have to make a pie special for you, Aza."

Its eyes lit up. "Really?"

"Really." Dub had a mischievous grin on his face. "After you get back with the boys, that is."

"Wait. After I what?" Aza asked.

Desi actually cracked a smile. "Aza can come with us?"

"Aza *will* go with you."

Wake snickered. "Looks like you really are our guide."

Aza groaned. "Fine."

"Good!" Ebbie clapped her hands. "Then let's all head to the connection. I think it's a good idea for you boys to see what happens."

The walk to where the islands would be connecting was a nice one. It was a shame that they couldn't spend a bit more time taking in the island, but maybe that was for the best.

Wake knew he and Desi were lucky to have bumped into such friendly creatures right away. If they had bumped into that farmer first, who knows what could have happened.

"If you make it to a connection point early, don't stand too close to the edge, especially if you're crossing just in time," Ebbie said as she gave the boys a light tug back.

"Why's that?" Wake asked.

"There's a bit of a shake as the islands start to come together and when they pull apart. The last thing you need is to fall into the sea."

The islands drifted closer and the shaking she was talking about began. It was enough to nearly throw the boys to their knees, but Ebbie and Dub kept them steady. The islands connected together and the shaking stopped.

Wake neared the point where the islands attached to one another. "So, that's it?"

"That's it." Ebbie nodded and pointed at a group of creatures crossing a few miles away. "Now everyone has an hour to cross for whatever reason, but if they aren't back in time, it'll be—"

"Where am I taking them?" Aza grumbled as it made its way over to the boys.

"Good question." Ebbie looked toward Dub.

"Well," He scratched his belly. "I'd say a good place to start would be up at Amphinara's tower." He pointed to a nearby tower that jutted out toward the sky. If Dub hadn't pointed it out, Wake would have just thought it was some kind of lighthouse, even if it did have an unnatural lean to it.

"Who's Amphi—whatever?" Wake asked.

"Amphinara." Aza corrected. "It makes sense. She's one of the oldest and wisest beings of this world. If she doesn't actually have Cerulea's artifact, she'll at least have an idea of where we can start our search."

Wake looked at Ebbie and hung his head. "This is goodbye, then?"

Ebbie shook a finger. "Goodbye *for now*. I'll make up a fresh pie from scratch when you boys get back, and we'll help you get everything in order to head home." She held out her arms and Desi and Wake gave her the biggest hugs they could muster. "If either of you ever gets into any trouble, you're always welcome to come back here for as long as you need. Understand?"

They nodded as they pulled away, and Dub cleared his throat. "You're getting yourself all worked up, Ebbie. Not long before the waterworks start."

"I can't help it!" Ebbie wiped a tear. "The islands can be a dangerous place and it's hard when you don't have someone to count on."

Dub plopped a hand onto her shoulder. "It's not like they don't have anyone to count on. They have each other. They always will. Plus they even have Aza to look out for them."

"Yippie." Aza rolled its eyes. "Adventure with the humans. That totally won't be a pain."

"One last thing before you go." Dub crouched in front of the boys. "Not everyone is going to be as—accommodating as Ebbie and me. You need to be careful who you trust."

Wake stuck a thumb up. "Stranger danger. Right, Desi?"

Desi nodded as Ebbie and Dub laughed. "Exactly."

Wake and Desi each gave Dub a hug and made their way onto the other island. It was strange that stepping over a tiny crack made everything feel different. The islands hadn't separated, but it already felt like they were miles away from safety.

Aza crossed the line with them. "Are you guys ready—" It waved its hands. "For the adventure of a lifetime?"

Desi rubbed his neck. "I just want to get home."

Aza's expression shifted from one of arrogance to one of understanding. "I know. We'll get you home quick." It waved to Ebbie and Dub, and then looked up toward the skyward tower. "Wave to them or they'll bawl later. We can make it to the tower by nightfall."

"Bye, Ebbie! Bye, Dub!" Desi said as they each waved. When they turned back, Aza had already set off, so they hurried after him.

Desi nudged Wake. "Do you think we can do this?"

"Of course we can." Wake gave him a playful nudge back. "It's just a couple of little artifacts. A day or so on the rest of the islands means we'll be home in a couple of days probably—if we don't fall too far behind."

"But what are we going to eat? The food Ebbie packed us isn't going to last that long."

Wake looked down at his satchel. "We'll figure it out. We've got Aza to help us anyway, and he's got to eat, right Aza?"

"Food?" Aza turned with wild eyes. "What about food?" The boys laughed. "What? Oh, forget it. Let's get to that tower."

For a completely different island, Cerulea sure didn't feel all that different. If anything, maybe it felt a little less tropical, and a little more ancient. The dense trees didn't let in much light, and the ground was made up of more loose dirt than on Mahlurma.

As they neared the tower, Wake felt a sharp pinch on his arm.

"Ow! What the—" Whatever had bitten him had drawn blood. It was a small bite, but there were some clear teeth-marks.

"You okay?" Desi asked as he inspected the bite.

"I don't know what it was, but it really hurt." He wiped the blood away. "It's okay now, I think."

"Let me have a look." Aza trudged over and pulled his hand down so it could see the bite on his arm. "Looks like a fly-gator bite."

The boys each raised an eyebrow. "A what?"

"There, see?" Aza pointed at a tiny alligator, no bigger than a bumble-bee, with a pair of wings on its back. "Fly-gators. Little jerks. Just give it a swat, and it'll leave you alone. We're probably just near a nest."

Desi stared at it as it flew close. "That's an alligator. Those are supposed to be huge."

"Alligator?" Aza crossed its arms. "If fly-gators were any bigger, the islands would be in big trouble." It flew near Aza and it gave the fly a good whack.

When they finally made it to a break in the trees, a whole new village was in view. This wasn't like the last one with crude huts and farms. This was a city, complete with stone walkways and plenty of shops. If the village was lively, this city was an all-out party.

It was almost disappointing that the tower was right in front of them. Wake got excited to see what insanity this new place had in store, though he figured Desi didn't share that same enthusiasm.

"You two need to stick close to me while we're here, okay?" Aza peered around as it stepped onto the stone path of the city. "All the islands are pretty similar in that most folks don't look too fondly at humans."

Wake nodded. "This Amphibaba—"

"Amphinara," Aza corrected.

"Am-phin-ara?" Wake asked, and Aza nodded. "Jeez, that's hard to say. Amphinara. What's she like?"

"To be honest—" Aza put a paw on the tall stone tower as it reached it. "I've never met her. I'd just suggest being on your best behaviour. There's no telling what she could do to the both of you if you step out of line."

Desi gulped. "Thanks for letting us know that right before we climb her tower."

49

"Had to be sometime," Aza said with a shrug. "Oh, and there's probably gonna be a thing—a strange thing —I don't know if it's real or not, but if you notice anything weird about her, don't mention it."

"Got it." Wake walked up to the large wooden door. "Should I knock?"

Just let yourselves in, my dear.

His eyes went wide because there wasn't anyone who could have said that. No one was near them. It didn't even sound like the voice was spoken. It felt like it was inside of Wake's head.

He looked up. "Amphinara?"

Don't dawdle. I haven't got all night. Come in.

"You guys can hear that, right?" Desi nodded with his mouth wide-open. "Good. At least I'm not crazy."

Wake took a breath and opened the door. The tower was pitch black. It was so dark that he could barely see more than two steps past the doorway. He took a few steps inside and the others followed.

The door swung shut and Desi yelped.

"Desi, you okay?"

"Yeah—just—just the d-dark."

My apologies my dear.

SNAP!

The darkness melted away and the three of them were standing in the middle of a misty workshop. There were brooms sweeping without anyone holding them, bubbling cauldrons, and even what looked to be a tiny fairy flying around.

The room didn't smell the way he thought it might at a glance. Exotic scents or maybe even something a little stinky might have made sense with all the strange bubbling liquids. Instead, the room had a sweet citrusy smell.

"What just happened?" A window caught Wake's eye. They weren't on the ground anymore. They were at the top of the tower. "How did we—what?"

"Welcome, welcome!" The voice Wake had heard in his head boomed. "Been a while since I've seen a pair of humans. I'd almost forgotten your kind is just bigger sprites without wings."

Wake whirled around and stared at a massive frog-woman. She was so big that it looked like she might have been trapped in the tower. Her large beady eyes and puffy cheeks gave her a cutesy appearance, but the thick grey beard she sported confused him.

"Amphinara?"

Chapter 8:
A Trip To The Market

"Amphinara, that is what some call me, yes," The froggy wizard said as she twirled a slimy finger through her long beard. "Others call me by my full title."

Something was telling Wake that the thing Aza said not to mention had to be her thick beard.

"Your full title?" Wake asked.

"Amphinara The Occasionally Wise, at your service." Her throat expanded, nearly knocking over some of her magical items and a stack of books. "What can I do for such strange travellers? Not many humans walking around with Kolas."

"Trust me," Aza said as it raised its hands. "It's not by choice—oh, mighty frog-wizard."

"FROG—WIZARD?!" Amphinara looked like she was about to swallow Aza whole. "Hush, you. All things are a choice." She composed herself and turned her attention back to the boys. "Why are you here?"

Desi nudged Wake forward, and he cleared his throat. "We're trapped here—"

"Trapped, you say? That's certainly not good."

"No, and we're trying to find a way home to—"

Amphinara clapped her hands. "Oh, a way home. You're just two little heroes on a quest to find home. How adorable."

"Right, and to do that we need to—"

"Become formidable warriors? Grow wings? Sprout a couple of gills?"

Her continuous interruptions were getting on Wake's nerves. Desi must have known that because he put a hand on his shoulder. It didn't matter. Rude interruptions were one of Wake's pet peeves.

"NO!" Amphinara looked both surprised and impressed by Wake's outburst. "Sorry."

"I think what he means is—" Desi stepped in front of Wake. "We're looking for five artifacts so we can get home. We were told you might be able to help us find them."

"Ah. You truly are humans seeking passage back to your world then." She let out a slight croak. "I can point you in the direction of your next artifact right here on this island—if you do something for me in return first."

"Anything," Wake piped up. "Whatever it takes."

Amphinara narrowed her eyes at him. "Be careful with your words boy. You certainly wouldn't be saying that if I told you I wanted your companions for my supper, would you?"

"I—"

"Would you?"

"No. I wouldn't."

"I didn't think so."

"What do you need us to do?" Desi asked.

"I have a list of sorts. A list of things I need for a very special trio of potions." Amphinara lashed her tongue toward a nearby table to retrieve a piece of parchment. She took the slobbery piece of paper in her hands. "If you hurry, you may be able to get everything you need tonight."

Desi took the list from her. "I—uh—"

"What is it?"

"I don't know what half of this stuff is."

Aza climbed up to Desi's shoulder and snatched the list. "Feet, warts, residue, petals—" It trailed off as it muttered to itself. "Yep, this is all doable. Pretty sure I saw a stall with some of this when we were outside, but I know a few shops we can visit."

"Excellent." Amphinara croaked happily. "Then be on your way! The potion will need the night to brew, so chop-chop."

"Wait," Wake said as he took a look at the list. "We don't have any money. How are we supposed to get all that?"

"I'll handle all of that," Aza headed back toward the door. "Come on."

As Wake and Desi followed behind, Amphinara cleared her throat. "I forgot to mention one thing."

"What's that?" Wake asked.

"That trio of potions? I will need someone to test them for me."

"That wasn't part of the—"

SNAP!

In an instant they were all back in that dark room, the only light was that of the moon piling through the open door.

"So that was—something."

"Sh!" Aza brought one of its claws to its mouth. "Not here." The boys followed him out of the tower and into the bustling streets. "Heads down. Don't need anyone freaking out about the humans."

Desi looked like he had something to say, so Wake gave him a nudge. "What is it?"

"I'm just wondering—remember what Ebbie and Dub said about strangers? I know they told us to find her, but do you think we can trust her? She seems a little—"

"Super weird?"

"Really weird."

Aza shook a finger. "I know she's a bit strange, but she's trustworthy. I'm not too sure about the potions, but we'll cross that island when we connect with it."

"Where are we headed?" Desi asked.

"Toward the market. Cerulea has the best fresh market out of any of the travelling islands. Voxal may have more markets to offer, but you've gotta inhale about a ton of smog just to get to any of them in the first place."

They passed a group of fish-creatures all giving them the stink-eye. One looked to be part shark, while another might have been part pufferfish. At first, Wake almost thought one was a normal human until he glanced at the set of gills along his neck.

"The people here don't seem too friendly," Wake said as he put his head down. "Is it really a good idea for us to come along into any shops?"

"We'll only need to go into two places, the rest we can snag from the stalls. We'll play it by ear. You two almost screwed up with the farmer, so if you screw this up, I'll make you sit in an alley or something."

Desi gave a thumbs up. "Works for me."

Wake rolled his eyes. "That would work for you. You could at least try to have fun. Do you think we're going to accidentally get stuck in some crazy world every week?"

"I don't care. I just want to get home and sleep in my bed without worrying whether or not something is going to try to take a bite out of me."

"Zip it you two," Aza said as they waded into the crowded market. "Unwanted attention."

There were strange creatures every way the boys looked. Some of them were buying even stranger things. Some things Wake couldn't even hazard a guess as to the purpose of. Who knew why a fish-man would want to buy what looked like a jar of bird talons?

The market exuded a kind of energy that the boys liked. The bright lights made it feel inviting despite some rather gruesome beings. There was even strange music coming from somewhere even deeper in the city.

Aza lifted a fold of belly fat to reveal a small belt. It pulled a couple of small silver coins out and tossed it to a multi-headed deer with a bunch of chefs' hats on.

"These are great." It snatched a couple of skewers with some kind of meat on it and handed one to each of the boys. "Only available here in Cerulea."

Wake gave the strange meat a sniff. Whatever it was, it reminded him of sizzling steaks. The closer he looked at the bits of meat, the less desirable it became. They were hunks of meat, but they looked to be tiny lizards.

Desi popped one in his mouth, and the sounds of it crunching curled Wake's lip. "Is it good?"

"Yeah." Desi shrugged. "It's kind of like when mom cooks beef too long, but it's crunchy." Crunchy was not an appealing way to describe a piece of meat. Desi laughed at Wake's disgusted look. "Look's like I'm the adventurous one for once, huh?"

He rolled his eyes and popped a piece into his mouth. The texture wasn't the greatest, but the burst of flavour was unlike anything he'd had before. It was better than any meat he'd ever eaten.

"Hey," Wake popped another piece into his mouth. "This isn't half bad."

The trio continued through the market and gawked at the various bustling stalls. There were some creatures playing huge instruments neither of the boys had seen before. They resembled horns, but they were incredibly long, and the neck of each of the instruments was curled.

"Here." Aza tugged Wake's shirt. "We can get some of what we need in here."

Desi looked up at a sign reading, *General Store*. "I guess even monsters can make their own stores."

"Watch who you're calling a monster, human," Aza said as it opened the door. "Plenty of us *monsters* would just as soon call you humans monsters with everything you've done around here."

They all wandered into the shop and looked around at the strange goods. Wake had only ever been to a general store once, but it was just an old building in a tiny town. This shop was huge, and it looked brand new.

"What have humans done that's so bad?" Wake asked as he stared at a case filled with different furs.

"Yeah. We aren't so bad. We even landed on the moon once," Desi added.

"Landed on the moon? What are you—" Aza scratched its head. "Never mind. Ms. Ebbie and Dub told you about Conah? That's what humans have done. Voxal was a beautiful island—one of the happiest of all the islands—that is until humans started coming around. Now most people who spend more than a day there, end up sick from the disgusting smog."

"Oh." Desi grabbed a small cup from a shelf. "If it helps, I don't even know how to make any smog—" A slimy green tentacle wrapped around Desi and hoisted him into the air. "WHOA!"

"Little humans looking to steal from me again?" A huge squid-creature said from behind the counter. Desi started to speak, but the creature tightened its grip and he cried out in pain.

Wake shot forward. "Let him go!"

The creature launched another tentacle toward Wake, but Aza stepped in the way. "Rin, relax. These two are good kids. Put Desi down or I'm going to make sure Ms. Ebbie stops sending snacks to this part of Cerulea."

"Aza." Rin looked surprised. "Desi?" It pulled Desi closer and squinted at him. "Desi is not the name of the human that stole from me." It glared at Wake. "Who are you? Was it you? What's your name?"

"My name's Wake. I've never even been to a place like this before, so it couldn't have been me."

Rin dropped Desi to the floor. "Keep your filthy hand off of my goods."

"Y-yes, sir." Desi nodded.

"You two sure are a pain in the butt." Aza took a deep breath. "Now that the crisis is averted—" It handed the list to Rin. "Got ourselves a little list here. It's for Amphinara. You wouldn't happen to be stocked up would you?"

Rin took a closer look at the list. "You're in luck. Fresh shipments from Flurris just the other day."

"That's cool," Desi said as he approached the counter. "You guys all trade with each other? All the different islands I mean."

Rin nudged Desi backward. "Of course we do." His tentacles shot off into the store. One rushed by Wake so fast, he was thankful he hadn't taken a tiny step to the left. "For Amphinara, the ingredients are on the house."

After a few moments, all of Rin's tentacles returned with almost everything that was on the list. It opened up a brown paper bag with a free tentacle and started placing everything inside.

"Great! We'll only need to make one more stop." Aza grinned.

"Alright!" Desi pumped a fist. "Two artifacts in one day. Easy."

"Don't get too excited," Wake said as he took the packed bag from Rin. "We still gotta find the rest of the ingredients, wait for the potions to brew, and then we have to try them."

"Oh, yeah."

"There's no telling what the potions might do either."

"Wake's right," Aza nudged him. "But that doesn't mean you can't be excited. A step in the right direction is always something to celebrate." It headed toward the door. "Thanks for the help—and not squishing the life outta the boys, Rin."

Rin waved his tentacles. "Don't mention it. See to it that they aren't unaccompanied. You don't want to know what I was ready to do."

The boys hurried behind Aza. They really didn't want to find out what Rin meant. That's without mentioning that Rin wasn't even one of the scariest creatures they'd seen. There was always room for things to get a lot worse.

They headed back out to the busy market, but Aza led them into a quiet alley. "The other place we need to visit is around the corner." It stared at Desi. "I'll be going in alone."

"Aw, man."

"We won't touch anything this time." Wake offered.

Aza shook its head. "I just need you two to stay out of trouble while I'm inside. I'll just be a few minutes and then we're going to head right back to Amphinara's."

"How much trouble could we get in, in a few minutes?" Wake asked with a shrug.

"You two?" Aza gave him a dull look. "You do realize you were about to be de-boned by Rin back there, right?" It started toward the street. "No trouble."

Desi and Wake shook their heads. "No trouble."

For some reason, there was a bit of an awkward feeling in the air. Maybe being directly told to avoid trouble just made the pull of mischief even stronger.

"I wonder if anyone's gonna believe us when we get

back." Wake sighed and gave an empty bucket a little kick. "Probably not, huh?"

"Probably not." Desi stretched. "Might as well give our legs a break while we have the chance." He attempted to scoot his butt onto a barrel, but the barrel must have been completely empty. When he put his weight on it, it tipped to the side, sending him crashing to the ground, and sending the barrel out to the street.

Wake groaned. "Desi—"

"Oops."

"You alright?"

He rubbed his butt. "Yeah, I'm fine."

There was a commotion out on the street, and before anything else happened, Wake knew they had found their trouble.

"HEY! Who's throwing barrels around here?" A gruff voice shouted. "Someone could really get hurt!"

"Great." Wake scowled at Desi. "Remember a minute ago when Aza said no trouble? Then we both agreed, *no trouble?*"

"Sorry."

The outline of a brutish figure stepped into the end of the alley.

Wake clicked his tongue. "I have a feeling sorry isn't going to cut it." He yanked Desi to his feet and looked toward the figure. "Sorry about that, just an accident."

It stormed right up to Desi and hoisted him up against the wall. "What're two humans doing here?"

It was hard to tell what it was at a distance, but up close it would have been impossible to miss. It was a muscular whale, only a little bit smaller than the average person.

"We're just waiting for our friend," Desi squeaked out.

"Well, then I'll keep you company until your friend gets back." Wake watched the whale-creature's grip tighten on Desi.

Wake snatched the bucket he had kicked and whacked it over the whale's head.

"AH!" It dropped Desi. "You're gonna—"

Wake didn't want to stick around and find out what that creature had to say. He grabbed Desi and pulled him hard toward the opposite end of the alley. They rushed out to another section of the market, and tons of monstrous eyes fell on them.

"YOU LITTLE BRATS!" the whale shouted from the alley.

"What do we do?" Desi asked.

"We run." Wake pulled him again, this time in the direction of the woods that had those fly-gators.

They had to push past a few monsters and hop over a few shop stalls, which gave Wake a feeling that they were only making humans look worse. It's not like they had a choice, though. Get pummelled by a whale that could have been a professional wrestler or irritate a couple of people—Wake wasn't about to become a punching bag.

They wouldn't dare look back, but the clattering and loud gasps from behind them told each of the boys that the creature was still on their heels.

"Here!" Wake pulled Desi around a corner and pointed toward a fallen log with a fly-gator perched on it. "This looks familiar right?"

Desi scratched his head. "It's dark, but this is where you got bit by that alligator thing right?"

"Yeah, somewhere around here."

Desi looked back toward the whale. "What are we going to do?"

"Look around." Wake picked up a couple of rocks and handed a few to Desi. "We just need to find wherever their nest is."

"You think they're like bees? A nest in a tree?"

He shrugged. "We don't have a lot of other choices."

They both moved through the trees and searched as the whale's footsteps grew louder.

Desi tugged Wake's sleeve. "Up there." He pointed at a huge nest that was crawling with fly-gators. "That's gotta be it."

"Good job." He pulled Desi into a nearby bush as the whale broke through the trees. He set the bag filled with ingredients down and watched the creature.

"Where'd those little barrel-throwing brats get to?" The whale muttered.

Just a few more steps and it would be right under the nest.

Three more.

Two more.

One more.

"NOW!"

The boys shot up from the bushes and chucked the rocks toward the nest as hard as they could. Who's rock nailed the nest didn't matter. All that mattered was that one of them hit the mark, causing the nest to sway.

The whale laughed. "You kids can't even aim right!"

The nest ripped from the branch it was attached to and dropped right onto the whale's head. It broke open and the fly-gators swarmed it. Wake pulled Desi behind a tree in hopes that the fly-gators wouldn't pay any attention to them.

"AH! AH! AHHHH!" the whale screamed as he took off back toward the city.

The boys were out of breath, but that didn't stop them from celebrating with a high-five. After a few minutes in hiding, just to be sure the creature didn't return, the boys put some space between them and the fallen nest. It was a straight shot back to Amphinara's tower from there.

They looked through the bag of ingredients and waited for Aza by the base of Amphinara's tower.

Aza had to assume something had gone wrong and made its way back to the tower at some point. Whenever a creature wandered by, the boys would dip around to the opposite side of the tower, just to avoid any potential problems.

Aza came into view with another bag in hand and stormed toward the boys. "You were supposed to wait for me! What happened?"

Wake looked toward Desi and laughed. "Long story."

Aza groaned. "You two are going to be the death of me."

Chapter 9:
A Potion That Can't Work

"Back with the ingredients so soon?" Amphinara looked impressed. "You boys really must be in quite the hurry."

"We've already been gone a long time," Wake said. "Our mom is totally gonna kill us."

Her neck bulged as she croaked with laughter. "A real mother would do no such thing."

"Well, she'll be really mad," Desi said.

"Naturally. I trust you managed to gather all of the ingredients?"

"No thanks to these two." Aza growled. "I'm out here getting everything on your list while these two are almost getting squished and chased around the city."

"Yes. I thought it was you two causing all that ruckus." Amphinara gazed at the window. "I'll be sure to make an example of the brute who chased you."

"Really? Are you sure? We did kinda hit him with a barrel."

"But it was an accident?" She brought her hands to the sides of her head. "I can see it. It was, wasn't it?" The boys nodded as she continued. "Then he should never have chased you. I'll make him spend a day as a rather large aquavine or something. That sounds nice."

"What do we do now?" Wake asked as he set all the ingredients out next to a cauldron.

"This is my favourite part," Amphinara croaked. "Toss all the ingredients in, and give it fifteen stirs. No more, no less."

"Fifteen stirs," Wake muttered to himself. He and Desi tossed all the ingredients in and he gave the cauldron the necessary stirs.

With each full circle of the cauldron, the bubbling liquid changed colours. On the fifteenth stir, the liquid settled into a light blue colour.

"Didn't you say all of this was for three potions?" Wake put his hands on his hips. "We just used all the ingredients."

"We weren't supposed to like, get three of everything, were we?" Desi asked.

Amphinara laughed. "Relax, my child. You just leave that to me. This brew must settle for the night, and then I can separate it into three potions." Her tongue shot out of her mouth and smacked into a huge wardrobe. It popped open and three beds, perfect sizes for each of them, fell out. "You three may stay the night, and we'll get to everything in the morning."

"Thanks, Amphinara." the boys said with a smile.

Amphinara had already shut her eyes and begun to snore. Aza shrugged and crawled into its small bed. The boys looked at each other, both feeling just how tired they were for the first time. It was a long excitement-filled day.

They each crawled under the covers of their beds and the next time they blinked their eyes open, it was the next day. It didn't even feel like they had slept at all. It really was nothing but a blink, but they were fully rested.

Wake sat up and stared at Desi as he did the same. "Weird." The scent of chalk filled his nose. Whatever was brewing, it probably didn't taste great.

"That was the best sleep I've had in a long time," Desi said with a stretch.

"No kidding. I can't even remember falling asleep."

"Enchanted beds." Aza chuckled. "You plop down in one and you don't even need to try to sleep. You just open your eyes and it's morning. Neat, huh?"

Wake ran a hand along the bed. "Super neat." He looked over at Amphinara, she had become much smaller and thinner than last night. She was hunched over the cauldron. "Amphinara? You've changed—"

She spun around and giggled. "Of course I changed. I get bored of looking one way for too long." She ran a finger through her beard.

"Not everything's changed." Aza laughed.

"What do you mean?"

"Nothing. Don't worry about it." Aza jumped up and down to peer into the cauldron. "You need us to help with anything?"

She scooped some of the blue liquid into a small vial. "Everyone is well-rested I trust?" They all nodded. "Good. I will need each of you to try my potions."

She threw in a handful of some kind of powder and the cauldron exploded in her face. She wafted the smoke away and poured a red liquid into a vial. The chalk smell morphed into the sweet smell of buttery popcorn.

Desi curled a lip. "It's not gonna turn us into anything, right?"

"Yeah, I don't think our mom would be too happy if we turned into some kind of weird multi-legged creature," Wake said as he got a closer look at the cauldron.

Amphinara lashed her tongue toward a bowl of fruit and tossed a spit-covered apple into the cauldron. "You fear I couldn't turn you back to normal if I changed your form?" She stirred the cauldron and it shifted into a dark green.

"I'm sure you could turn them back to normal just fine. Right, boys?" Aza asked.

"Right." they replied, not entirely sure if that was the truth.

She poured the last of the liquid into a third vial and held all three out toward them. "Pick whichever one you'd like."

"How do they taste?" Desi asked.

The unpleasant odour of the last potion had Wake wondering the exact same thing.

Amphinara brought a finger to her cheek. "That's a good question."

Wake and Desi waited for an answer that never came. "Are you going to tell us?"

"Tell you what?"

"What they taste like."

"Oh!" Amphinara looked down at the vials. "I have no idea. Never made these potions before."

Wake grabbed the red potion. "So we're supposed to test a bunch of potions you've never tried to make before?"

"If you want my artifact, yes."

Aza grabbed the dark green potion, leaving the blue one for Desi. Even though they all came from the same cauldron, the potions had different properties. Wake's had bubbles rising to the surface, Aza's looked like a thick slime, and Desi's looked like a little vial of juice.

"Who wants to go first?" Aza asked. Desi and Wake stared at it. "You're kidding."

"You're the guide." Wake shrugged. "Guide us."

"I can't guide you through drinking a potion!"

Desi snickered. "You're *so* brave, Aza."

"That's funny coming from you!" Aza growled. It flicked the top of the vial open and held it up. "I hope it tastes like eucalyptus." It started to drink the potion.

"No—" Amphinara croaked. "I don't remember that ever being a potion flavour."

Whatever the potion tasted like, it caused Aza to gag. Everyone backed up in case it started to throw up, but instead, it let out a little burp.

"Is something supposed to happen? I don't feel any different. I just feel like there's some slime sitting in my gut now."

She held up a finger. "Wait for it."

———

Nothing.

"Hmm. That's strange. I was pretty sure you would end—" Aza started to balloon in size. "There it is!"

"What's happening to me? I can't feel my toes."

"You're getting huge!" Desi gawked.

"You're fine." She slapped Aza's flailing hand. "You're just going to grow a bit."

"How much is a bit?" Aza asked. Amphinara replied with a shrug. "Uh-oh."

Aza grew to roughly the same size that Amphinara had been the previous night. Something about it was almost cute, like someone over-filled a stuffed animal. It seemed the same, aside from the deep breaths it was taking.

"My potion worked perfectly," Amphinara smirked.

"Were you worried it wouldn't?" Aza asked in a panic.

"Of course not. That one wasn't even the hard one to brew."

That sounded strange considering none of the potions looked particularly hard to brew. Wake figured there had to be some kind of extra magic going on that he didn't know about. There had to be more to making a potion like that than just tossing some talons and fur into water.

Wake flicked Aza's blob of a belly. "How do you feel?"

"The same, but bigger."

"How do we get him back to normal? We're still gonna need his help, and getting around with something this big might be trouble."

"I suppose I have seen enough." Amphinara picked up a large staff. "Shmuh-Shmuh-Shmuh-HA!" She struck Aza in the middle of its belly, sending it flying around the room like a popped balloon.

"AHHHHHH!" Aza shrieked as it flew around.

Wake knew that he and Desi were both thankful they hadn't picked that potion. Seeing Aza fly around was kind of funny, but he knew he couldn't laugh. Neither of the boys had taken their potion yet, and there was no telling what kind of changes they would make.

Aza slammed into the wardrobe and hit the ground. "Ow. I am never—ever—testing a potion for you again."

Amphinara set her staff back down. "Don't be so dramatic. You're fine."

It got up and patted his body. "I guess you're right, but the point still stands."

"Coward."

"I'd be happy to be a coward if I never had to try another potion."

"Sh!" She turned her attention to the boys. "Next!"

"Do you want me to go first?" Wake asked.

Desi shook his head. "I think waiting would feel even worse." He flicked open the vial and slurped back the blue liquid. "Huh."

"What? Do you feel any different?"

"No. It tasted like blueberries."

Wake remembered an old story. "He's not going to turn into an actual talking blueberry now, is he?"

Amphinara gave him a confused look. "You humans sure are strange. Try a little run."

"A little—" Desi bolted to the other end of the room in a blur. "Run." He stared at his feet. "What the—"

She clasped her hands together. "Two for two! I truly am the wisest in the land—occasionally." Desi gave her an excited look. "Well, go on. Take a quick run."

Desi bolted out of the tower and Wake rushed to the window. He was able to see the blurred trail and rushing winds Desi was creating as he ran through the busy streets. As quickly as he had left, he appeared back in the tower.

"This-is-so-awesome." Desi was even speaking faster than his usual chatterbox speed. "Can-we-have-a-couple-of-these? That-would-be-super-awesome."

"No." Amphinara grabbed her staff again. "Shmuh-Shmuh-Shmuh-HA!" She tapped each of Desi's feet. "Special order. The last thing any of the inhabitants of these islands need is two little humans sprinting through their homes."

"Is that it? The speed's gone?" Wake asked.

"Good question. Give running another go, child."

"I think so. I already feel different, but I don't know what it is that feels different. Here goes." Desi shrugged and took a few quick steps at his normal speed before tripping to the floor. "Yep. It wore off alright."

Wake laughed. "Looks like that potion might actually be good for speed *and* balance."

Amphinara hopped to a nearby desk and scribbled something down. "Noted. You're next. Best for last."

Wake held the vial to his lips. "Best? Something you want to tell me about this one? This isn't about to be the *occasionally* in your name, right? I'm not going to turn into a dinosaur or something? I wouldn't be mad about becoming a T-rex."

"Dinosaur?" Amphinara and Aza looked equally confused.

"Here goes nothing." Wake hoped the red liquid would taste like cherries or fruit-punch, but instead it tasted more like medicine. "Ugh. If the effect has to do with the taste, I'm not so sure I'm in for something fun."

Amphinara picked up her staff and did a circle around him. "How do you feel?"

"Uh. Completely normal actually."

"Really?"

Wake raised an eyebrow. "Should I not feel completely normal?"

Amphinara started to poke and prod him. "It's a sign of something."

"A sign of something? A sign of what?" Wake looked toward Desi and Aza. "Do I look any different?"

Desi gave him a puzzled look. "Maybe—maybe you're a little taller?"

"I don't feel taller."

Amphinara got in his face and stared into his eyes. "You're completely fine?"

Wake inched backward. "Completely."

"You're sure?" She inched forward. "Nothing is off at all?"

Wake looked himself up and down and tried to focus on how his body was feeling, but nothing felt out of the ordinary. "I'm sure."

She tapped his chest with her staff and smiled. "Good."

"Good?"

Aza climbed up Desi and clung to his back. Desi gave him a confused look. "You know, you are way lighter than you look."

"First of all, rude." It looked from Desi to Amphinara. "Second, is it one of those potions that does nothing?"

"You mean coloured water?" Desi asked.

"Not a potion that does nothing." Amphinara whipped around. "A potion that can't work."

71

Wake blinked in confusion. "I'm gonna need some kind of help here."

"It's simple." Amphinara tossed her staff and stared at her cauldron. "The potion was either going to be a deadly poison, or it wouldn't do anything at all."

"Wait, you had me test if that was poison?" Wake asked. "Why would you even need something like that?"

Amphinara croaked. "You'd be surprised."

"We seem to be hearing that a lot."

Desi moved to the cauldron. "Ms. Amphinara, we did everything you asked. Could you please tell us about that artifact now?"

She ran her fingers through her beard. "I suppose." She pulled a glowing key from the inside of her robes and tossed it to Wake. "You boys take good care of that."

It was strange that such a simple little key was some kind of artifact, but the simpler the better.

"Thank you, Amphinara," Wake said with a bow.

"A bow? I'm a tower dweller, not royalty." She headed toward her bed and laid down. "You said you wanted to know if I knew where any of the others were, right?"

"Yes, please. We kind of have an idea of a few, but anything helps."

"Flurris, an artifact guarded in amongst a sea of treasure. Mulos, a prize found within veiled evil. Voxal, your journey's end begins at the tippy-top." She stretched out on the ground. "That's all I can tell you."

Aza looked at Wake. "Got all that?"

He nodded. "Easy."

"Good, good." She waved her hand. "Now begone with you. You have quite a long way to travel if you hope to make it to the Flurris crossing."

They all headed toward the door and Desi waved. "Thanks, Amphinara."

"Good luck, my child. *You* will need it."

Chapter 10:
The Plot to Rob a King

Amphinara wasn't kidding about the long trip to Flurris. They were lucky that the tower was so close to where they had left Mahlurma, but the uneventful trek across Cerulea left them barely enough time to make it over the crossing before the islands parted.

As they approached, the islands started pulling apart, forcing them all to make a small leap across to Flurris. They all dropped to the ground and tried to catch their breath.

"Let's—never—cut it—that close—ever again," Wake said through heavy breaths.

"Don't have—to tell me—twice," Desi replied. "We would have been fine—if Aza didn't need so many pit stops."

"It's not—my fault—" Aza held a claw in the air. "I have smaller—organs—which means I need—to tinkle more."

Wake started to laugh, and then Desi joined in. Before long, all three of them were laughing at the absurdity of their adventure.

They all got up and dusted themselves off, while Aza climbed onto Wake's back. "You know, you two aren't so bad for a couple of humans."

"You *are* weirdly light." Wake chuckled.

"Still rude."

"Well, we've never met a koala, but you're probably cooler than most."

"Kola. No idea what a *koala* is."

"Yeah, yeah, yeah."

Desi took a deep breath. "Do you have any idea where this castle is supposed to be?"

It looked around. "Use your eyes, kid." Aza pointed to an extravagant castle far off in the distance. "Flurris Castle—right there."

Wake couldn't blame Desi for not seeing it. The castle was so far off in the distance that it almost blended in with the surrounding forests. The only reason it stood out was the gorgeous shining lake that surrounded it.

"Oh, great. More walking," Desi moaned.

Wake headed in the direction of the castle. "What did you expect when Dub told us we'd have to go to different islands?"

"I dunno. More cars?"

"Could you imagine that huge farmer from Mahlurma driving?"

Desi shuddered. "I never want to picture that."

"Car?" Aza said as it looked between the boys.

"I guess you guys probably don't have those here, huh?" Desi asked.

"Actually, we do."

"Excuse me?" Wake stopped and stared at Aza "You mean we could have gotten Dub to drive us around or something?"

"Him? Behind the wheel?" Aza chuckled. "There are lots of cars on Voxal, that's the only place that has 'em. We could always keep our eyes out for a cart, though."

They walked through another line of trees and came to a path that winded through a few small plains and into a distant forest. It looked like the quickest route was going to be heading through the ominous woods.

"We've got a long way to go." Wake looked back to the castle. "Think we'll make it before it gets dark?"

"Depends how often Aza needs to tinkle." Desi snickered.

"Alright, I take back what I said about you two not being so bad."

The boys laughed as they crested a hill, but Wake shushed Desi when he heard a distant bumping.

"What?" Desi asked.

Wake smiled. "Ask and you shall receive."

"What are you talking about?"

"Tell me that doesn't sound like a cart."

"A cart? I don't hear any—" A wooden cart came over the hill. "Oh, that cart."

Aza hopped off Wake and jumped around in the middle of the road. "Hey! Stop!"

Wake wasn't sure what he should have pictured when he thought of some kind of animal-drawn cart on the island. He never could have pictured what they saw. Rather than cows or horses pulling the cart, it was being pulled by two huge ostriches with dark green fur and snow-white skin.

The cart pulled to a stop and the head of a large golden retriever stuck out from behind the ostriches. "Hello! Need ride?"

"Thanks for stopping, friend," Aza said as it climbed onto the cart.

Wake blinked at the dog dressed in tattered brown clothes. "Why wouldn't there be talking dogs here?"

Desi tapped his shoulder. "I think it's driving the cart too."

"Of course Shof drives cart," the dog said. "You humans coming with Shof?" The boys shrugged and climbed into the back of the cart with another strangely ordinary person. "Where headed?"

"To the castle. Are you headed that way?" Aza asked.

"To castle, no. In castle direction, yes. Shof will take you to other edge of Living Forest," Shof said as he pointed a furry paw toward the dark forest up ahead. "I'm Shof. Quiet stranger is Twig. Who are you?"

"I'm Wake." He pointed to Desi and Aza. "That's my brother Desi, and that's Aza."

"Aza! I like that name!"

Aza gave Wake a smug look. "Finally, someone who shows me a little respect."

Wake ignored him and turned his attention to the stranger named Twig. "Twig, right?" He nodded. "I don't know if this sounds weird or not, but you look really—"

"Human?"

"Yeah."

He didn't just look human. He looked like some of the cool kids from Wake's school. Twig couldn't have been much older than him.

After Twig leaned forward, a bunch of tails fell to either side of him. "I get that a lot. Got some human, got some fox."

"I don't think I wanna know how that works."

"One like me is born every thousand years, or at least that's what I've been told."

Desi stared at him in awe. "Cool."

"That's a different reaction."

"How do most people react?"

"Like I'm a freak."

Twig was far from someone Wake would call a freak. He had long and angular features that made him resemble a fox, but his thin leather garb really made him look cool. He looked like the kind of person Wake would want to dress up as for Halloween.

Wake and Desi gave each other a look. "That's how everyone's been looking at us since we got here. We'd never do that to someone else."

"Glad to hear it." He looked off toward the castle. "Your furry friend said you were headed for the castle? What for?"

"We're after an artifact that's being held in the castle. We need it so we can get home."

Twig's ears twitched when he mentioned the artifact. "Really? You guys just planning on walking in and asking the greedy hog for it?"

Wake rubbed the back of his neck. "I guess we haven't really thought about that." He watched the wheels of the cart spin. "Looks like we'll have lots of time to think about that. We aren't going all that fast."

Shof spun around with his tongue sticking out. "You want go fast?"

Everyone stared at him. "I mean, sure. If we can go a bit faster, why not?"

"Hold on." Without looking forward Shof snapped his reins on the ostriches and they extended huge wings.

"Uh. Aren't ostriches flightless birds? I feel like I read that once," Desi said as he gripped onto the side of the cart.

The ostriches flapped their wings and the cart shot into the air behind them. In moments, they had taken to the sky, and yet, that still wasn't the strangest thing to happen to them during their short adventure.

Wake grabbed onto a raised section of the cart. "They are flightless birds, but is it really so hard to believe they can fly here?" He raised an eyebrow at Desi. "We just came from a bearded-lady-frog's magic tower, we're travelling with a sassy blue-furred koala—Kola—whatever, and we are currently sitting in an ostrich pulled cart that is being driven by a literal golden retriever."

Desi closed his eyes tight. "Good point."

Wake looked over to Twig, but he just looked bored by the entire ride. Being used to the craziness of this world was one thing, but he figured being that high up would have been enough to make anyone a little nervous.

"We'll be to forest soon!" Shof said as his tongue flailed in the breeze. "We can't fly to castle. No place to land without making hogs angry. We have to go slow soon."

"The sooner we're back on the ground, the better," Aza said with a hand on its stomach.

Wake looked over the side of the cart and was amazed at just how far they'd managed to travel in such a short time. Who knew flying ostriches were so quick?

The height they were at really put just how tall the trees of the forest were into perspective. They were barely flying at a height greater than the tallest tree. The massive trunks reminded Wake of the huge fruit trees he never got to try and climb back on Mahlurma.

"Not big flyers?" Twig asked.

"What gave it away?" Desi asked with his eyes still shut.

"Nothing in particular." Twig chuckled. "It helps if you think of it more like floating."

Desi opened his eyes. "Like floating? Like, in water?"

"Exactly. Just focus on that and let your mind relax."

Desi shut his eyes. "Maybe next time."

Wake leaned back and tried to imagine himself floating on a windy lake instead. To his surprise, it got rid of the sick feeling in the pit of his stomach.

"This actually isn't that bad."

"I'm a lot of things, but a liar isn't one."

"Down, now," Shof said as he snapped the reins again.

The sick feeling came back as the birds launched back toward the ground. Wake couldn't help closing his eyes again, partially from the strong winds, but partially from the fear.

The boys were expecting some kind of crash, but they set back on the ground like they had never even left it. They both opened their eyes and they were back to their slow ride into the forest.

"Oh, hold up a second," Aza said as it pointed to a large pig. "I want to ask this guy a question." Shof pulled the cart to a stop beside a pig working away on some crops. He almost looked like he could have been Dub's cousin. "Excuse me? Farmer?"

"What do you want?" the pig oinked. "You can't have any of my crops."

The pig stretched his arms out like he was protecting his pitiful crops. He had a huge field, but there wasn't much growing. Either he had just finished harvesting most of his crops, or this pig was a really, really bad farmer.

His angry expression was enough to tell the boys that this pig had no relation to Dub at all.

"Whoa. Calm down, we don't want any of your crops. I was just wondering if you knew anything about the castle?"

The farmer's eyes got wide. "Know anything about the castle? Yeah," He became deadly serious. "Don't go there. King Hog is an evil, greedy pig."

"That's all well and good, but we *need* to visit the castle."

The farmer grunted. "He's banned all travellers from entering the castle tonight. His majesty is throwing a party."

"Hmm." Aza tapped Shof, and Shof put the cart back in motion. "Thank's anyway."

"Don't come back here. I don't want anyone near any of my crops."

"Yeah, yeah, yeah. Greedy pig."

"What are we going to do?" Desi asked. "We can't just wait until tomorrow. What if they don't want anything to do with us?"

Shof turned around. "We enter forest now. Everyone okay with that?"

Everyone nodded. "Thanks, Shof."

"You're welcome friends!"

The sun became blocked out by the tall leafy trees. They were barely into the forest, but Wake couldn't have blamed anyone for thinking that the sun was about to go down with how dark it was.

The trees were huge, but the branches hung low. It almost looked like the trees were holding hands with the way their branches wrapped around one another.

Twig tapped the boy's knees. "You boys need to get into the castle tonight? There's no way around it?"

"Unfortunately." Wake sighed. "Why? Do you know someone who could get us into this party?"

Twig narrowed his eyes. "Not exactly."

"What do you mean by that?"

"How do you guys feel about a little light theft?"

"We can't steal from a king!" Desi almost shouted.

"How else are you expecting to get anything from the king of the greedy pig island?" Twig leaned back. "You think if two humans waltz into a party uninvited and ask for a favour from the king, that he'll just grant it?"

Wake bumped Desi. "He makes a good point."

Wake was surprised to hear both Desi and Aza speak at the same time. "I knew you were going to say that."

"You said you're many things, but a liar isn't one, so I'm going to ask—are you some kind of professional thief?"

Twig stared at Wake before his expression broke into a smirk. "I am."

"You're headed to the castle anyway then aren't you?"

"I am."

"So if we just happened to tag along with you, it wouldn't be like *we* were breaking in and stealing. We'd just be following *your* lead."

"You know what?" Twig crossed his arms. "I'm impressed. The logic doesn't hold up the best, but it works for me."

"So that means you'll take us with you?"

Twig looked from Desi to Aza. "They don't seem too thrilled about the idea." He brought a hand to his chin. "More people could make things more difficult—"

"What are you doing?" Desi whispered to Wake.

Wake ignored him. "How good of a thief are you really?"

Twig leaned forward. "The best."

"The best?" He raised an eyebrow. "Well then, it sounds like you should be up for the challenge. You were practically offering to help us anyway."

Twig nodded to Aza. "The kid's good."

"A little too good," Aza groaned.

"Well?" Wake asked.

Twig gave everyone another look. "Let's do it."

The thumping of Shof's tail against the wood of the cart almost broke the seriousness of the situation. "My new friends are so brave!"

Chapter 11:
Through the Living Forest

For a thief, Twig was pretty easy to get along with. Wake, Desi, and Twig all chatted and laughed as they made their way through the forest. Shof and Aza were speaking in a more hushed tone, but it seemed like they were getting along just fine.

Who wouldn't get along with a walking, talking golden retriever?

"What was it like growing up on the islands?" Desi asked Twig.

"I don't know if I'm the best person to ask a question like that." He straightened the fur on one of his tails. "If someone can't spot my tails I get treated like a human, and I'm sure you two know exactly what that can mean."

"You have no idea," Wake replied.

"SH!" Aza snapped at them.

They all gave him a confused look. "What?"

"I'd at least expect you to know where we are, Twig."

He looked around. "The Living Forest. Don't tell me you really believe all those kid stories."

Shof cranked his neck to look back. "Not just stories."

"That's right." Aza nodded.

"Kid stories?" Wake took a look around. The trees were way bigger than any usual forest, but it didn't seem all that different otherwise. There was even a well-travelled road that they were on. "What do you mean?"

"They're pretty common stories that are told on just about every island. The stories are all about this forest and all the things that supposedly make it special."

"What kinds of things?" Desi asked.

"Everyone knows about the forest spirits."

"Forest spirits?"

Twig pulled a leaf from a tree that had a branch hanging extra low. "Yeah, but they aren't unique to this forest. They can be hard to come across especially for humans, but they can be found in every forest across the islands."

"Are they—evil spirits?" Desi asked, likely thinking of one of the creepy ghost movies the boys liked to sneak on late at night.

Twig laughed. "Far from it. I've actually only heard of them helping guide lost travellers out of the forests."

"So, there's no danger then? That's good."

"Well…"

Wake tapped Desi. "You had to ask, didn't you?"

"This forest is known as the living forest," Twig continued. "Because it's believed that the trees, the flowers, the grass—everything—is alive."

Wake raised an eyebrow. "But shouldn't nature be friendly?"

"It should," Aza cut in. "But as more humans found their way into our world, Voxal became the island of smog. A smog that choked out all of the land's nature."

"Nature talks," Shof barked.

"It does, indeed. Lately, there have been reports of the living forest lashing out violently against unaware travellers."

"You shushed us because we might get eaten by a tree or something?" Wake asked, not believing Aza.

"That's part of it." It gave him a serious look and then sighed. "Now then, let's keep it down until we reach the edge of the forest, alright? Last thing we need is to get Shof's cart torn apart by an angry tree seeking revenge for its fallen brother."

Wake ran his hand along the wooden bench he was sitting on. It was something he hadn't thought about, and likely never would have. That bench used to be a tree—maybe even one of the mighty trees in that forest. It was kind of like what Mac had said back on the farm, the tree gave itself to the inhabitants of the island.

He hoped the people of the island had treated it well.

"Think we'll see the forest spirits one day?" Desi asked Wake.

"Would you like to see them right now?" Twig asked. "I think I can get a few to come out."

"Really?" Desi spun around looking up to the trees. "Where?"

Twig pulled a small round item from his little bag. It looked like a small, smooth stone, just big enough to fit in the palms of his hands. As Twig handled it, Wake was able to see it was dotted with a bunch of small holes.

It was an instrument of some kind, but it was unlike any he'd ever seen.

"They love music. Watch the trees, especially the big empty branches," Twig said as he brought the instrument to his lips.

He fiddled with it for a moment. Blowing into a few of the different holes, seemingly to refresh his memory on the different notes. Each note felt familiar, but the sounds that flowed from the instrument were unique to this world.

Twig took a deep breath and began to play. The song was a hauntingly beautiful piece. It was the kind of music anyone would be more than happy to fall asleep to.

As he played, Twig nodded his head behind the boys.

They turned to see a tiny, chubby creature that seemed to be entirely wood and leaves, seated on an empty branch. As if they were hiding just out of sight, more poked their heads out from behind branches and through thick leafy branches.

The boys looked around to see what had to be hundreds, if not thousands of the small creatures happily swaying to Twig's song.

"There's—so many of them." Wake stared in wonder. "These are the embodiment of the nature here?"

Twig nodded as he played.

"That's enough of that," Aza said. "Those things give me the creeps."

Twig stopped playing and the spirits all disappeared. "Pretty cool, huh?"

The cart began to slow down, and Wake had a feeling he knew the reason. "Tinkle break, Aza?"

"You kids are getting to know me a little too well."

"I'm starting to think you just wanted to get rid of the spirits so you didn't wet yourself." Wake gave Desi a playful elbow and the two laughed at Aza.

"Very funny." It hopped out of the cart. "Take some time to stretch your legs while you've got it. I'll be right back."

Twig wiggled his fingers. "Or will you?"

Aza stuck its nose in the air. "I'll have you know I'm very in tune with nature." It pushed through a set of bushes.

The only sounds were those of the forest creatures doing—whatever it was strange forest creatures do.

Wake followed Twig out of the cart. "That instrument is really cool. Could you show me how to play?"

"Sure, why not?" He pulled out the instrument and looked back toward the cart. "Let's put a little distance between us and the cart so your friend won't get freaked out by the spirits again."

"Right." Wake waved at Desi. "We'll be right back. You okay to stay with Shof?"

"Uh—I dunno—"

"You'll be fine."

Wake followed Twig through a set of bushes to a small clearing. A cluster of small rocks would acted as a perfect group of chairs. They picked the two that were nearest to one another and took a seat.

"Basically, you blow into this part here, and you use your fingers to cover the holes to make different sounds." Twig demonstrated with a few notes from the song he had been playing. "You try." He handed the instrument to Wake.

It was a strange little thing. It almost looked like a tiny water jug or a baby's sip-cup. It felt right at home in his hands.

"It's kind of like the recorder, I guess."

"Recorder?"

"Oh—uh—it's like if you took this and stretched it out—kinda."

"You humans come from a strange land."

"We get that a lot." Wake positioned his fingers over the same holes Twig had. "Like this?"

"Yep. Now give it a try." Wake blew and the beautiful sound of the instrument danced amongst the trees. Twig helped him reposition his fingers to play the correct notes. "You've got it. Now put it all together and try it on your own."

"Already? I only practiced once."

"Your body will remember." He looked off in the direction of the cart. "Not like we have all day."

"Good point." Wake brought the instrument back to his lips and he took a breath.

"AHHH!"

Hearing anyone scream in the middle of the forest would have been bad enough, but that scream didn't come from just anyone.

That scream came from Desi.

Back in the direction of the cart, some kind of thick black smoke was rising into the air.

Wake sprinted back toward the cart with Twig on his heels. They made it back in view of the cart in time to see Desi being pulled up into the trees by a branch.

"WAKE! HELP!"

Wake stared up at Desi, Shof, and Aza, all being held by different tree branches. "What the heck?"

"It's the trees," Twig said with wide eyes. "They *are* alive."

A branch swung toward them, but they managed to hop out of the way in time. It smashed into the dirt path with a large **SLAM**. It curled on the ground, and shot toward Twig, wrapping around his ankle. It yanked him up into the air.

"Twig! What do we do?" Wake asked.

"Chop these trees into bits!" Aza shouted.

"I don't have an axe or anything."

"No, but he's got a knife!" Aza managed to stick a claw toward Twig.

"We can't hurt them!" Twig scoffed.

"Why not?"

He pointed toward the smoke rising in the distance. "The Hog King must have men burning trees to clear land." The branch waved Twig around as he struggled to avoid another branch. "It must have angered the forest."

"That still doesn't explain why you can't just cut the branches."

"That will—" He curled his body to avoid a branch swing. "Only make them—" He did it again just in time. "Even angrier. I don't think any of us want that."

Wake watched Shof struggle against the tight branches. "New tree friends—not very nice."

Another branch lashed out toward Wake but he ducked behind another tree. He looked down at Twig's instrument. "What if we could calm them down?"

"How the heck are we gonna do that?" Aza asked.

The second branch that was swinging at Twig managed to wrap him up. "That—would be worth—a try," Twig squeaked out.

Wake stepped back out and started to play the instrument.

One long note.

A second long note.

What was the third note?

What was the fourth note?

The fifth?

The sixth?

A branch wrapped around his ankle and pulled him to the ground. It dragged him along the dirt path, and soon he was going to be trapped in the trees with his friends. He had to remember the song.

"Wake! Relax! Clear your mind. I told you, your body remembers how to play it," Twig called down.

Wake closed his eyes and did what he could to shut out the rest of the world. He started to play once again, this time just allowing the music to flow. He played the same song Twig had played until he felt himself stop moving.

He popped an eye open to see that the tree had let go of him, but his friends were still being held. Some of the forest spirits had come out of hiding to hear the music.

"It's working," Wake muttered to himself.

"Keep playing!" Aza growled.

"Right." Wake continued playing what he could. When the trees still hadn't let go of his friends, he realized his nerves were making him play worse. He shut his eyes and cleared his head as he continued.

After what felt like forever, a slight tap stopped him. "Nice work, Wake."

It was Twig.

He was back on the ground.

Everyone was.

Wake looked around to see that the audience of the forest spirits had grown even greater than it had been back when Twig had been playing. Some started to clap while others danced and jumped around.

The forest had been appeased.

Twig and Desi helped him to his feet. "You guys all okay?"

Desi nodded. "Thanks to you."

"You're a natural," Twig flicked the instrument. "But I'm gonna need that back."

"Oh, yeah. Totally. I gotta get me one of those, just in case Desi and I have to walk through any more crazy forests."

"Yeah, yeah, yeah," Aza said as it and Shof hopped back in the cart. "Hate to break up the congratulations, but let's get back on our way so we can get the heck outta this forest."

Shof nodded. "Not far to castle."

They all climbed into the back of the cart as Shof snapped the reins. They were moving much faster, which wasn't all that surprising. Even big ostriches had to have been more than a little scared of the trees.

Wake nudged Aza. "You're holding it until we get to the castle."

"No kidding." Aza scoffed. "Pretty sure I won't need another tinkle break for a long while."

Wake turned back in time to see Twig give the instrument a bit of a shine with a cloth. "That must be pretty important to you, huh?"

Twig looked from the instrument to Wake. "It is. Not only are they pretty rare to come by, but it's also all I have left of my parents."

Wake hung his head. "I'm sorry."

"Nothing to be sorry for." He said with a shrug. "Who knows, if we see each other again after what I'm sure will be a hectic night at the castle, maybe I'll see if I can make another, just for you."

"Really?"

"No promises, but I'll see what I can do." He smiled at Desi. "I can even make one for you. When you make it home you can both annoy your family."

Desi beamed. "That would be awesome."

Twig messed up his hair. "Thought so."

"Shof pull up to bridge," Shof said, bringing everyone's attention to the long bridge leading to the castle.

The sun had begun to set, and it looked like some of the guests of the king's party were already arriving up ahead. The party was going to start at any moment.

Shof pulled the cart to a stop. "This where friends say goodbye?"

Everyone hopped out of the cart, and Wake headed to the front. "Yeah. This is our stop. Thanks for the ride, Shof."

"Shof always happy to help new friends." He smiled at Wake. "You be safe at castle. Hog King is real piece of work."

"We will." Wake pat one of the ostriches. "Will we see you again?"

"Shof always moving. Maybe—maybe not. Shof never forget friends. Don't worry."

Shof snapped his reins and waved as the ostriches pulled him back into the darkness of the forest.

Wake turned and stared at the Hog King's castle. "Time to get artifact number three."

Twig held up a hand. "Hold up. If the group of us are going to sneak in, we need to wait until it's dark. Then we can make our move."

Aza narrowed its eyes at Twig. "Remind me again why you're helping us?"

91

"The kids need an artifact, right?" He shrugged. "I need some gold. Shouldn't be too hard to grab both in the same trip."

"Alright." Aza looked like it didn't entirely believe him. "Let's get out of sight while we wait for the sun to set. Last thing we need is someone to spot us before we even try."

Desi tapped Wake's shoulder. "What kind of party do you think pigs throw?"

"I don't know, but hopefully it's a loud one."

Chapter 12:
A Flying Staircase

The group watched waves of regal pigs arriving for the party against the pink evening sky. The only cover they had was a thick set of bushes. Most of the pigs squealed with delight at being invited to the Hog King's castle, but a few sounded like they were only showing up so they could brag about it.

That was something that didn't make sense to Wake. Why bother going to some event that you don't really even want to attend?

Soon the land became engulfed in a dreamy darkness, with most of the light shining from the bright stars and enormous moon. The castle itself was so lit up that the light pouring from it could have acted as a beacon across the seas. Wake wondered if Ebbie and Dub would have been able to see the light from wherever Mahlurma was.

"You guys all set to get moving?" Twig asked as he checked all his gear. "Judging by that music, it looks like most people have arrived."

The music that bellowed from the castle was clear to them, even from across the bridge. It sounded similar to that stuffy old jazz music the boy's mother would listen to from time to time, only this sounded even more hectic. Brass horns squealed, almost as if they were a warning to stay away.

Wake grabbed a stick and swung it a couple of times. "I'm always ready." He faced Desi when he heard him laugh. "What?"

"I don't remember the last time you were this excited."

"How could I not be?" He tossed the stick. "We're going to break into some huge castle to nab an artifact from a greedy pig king."

"Hog King," Aza corrected.

"Whatever."

Twig held a hand up. "I don't want you guys getting too excited. Things could get really bad if we get caught. We need to stay out of sight. No one can know we were ever there."

"We'll be fine," Wake said as he pushed through the bushes. "We did a pretty good job of hiding from a giant. How hard could a couple of pigs be?" As he stepped out from the bushes he bumped into someone, sending both that person and himself to the floor. "Ow. I'm so sorry. Are you—"

A spear pointed right at his nose shut him up. "You'd dare harm Lady Kohdad?"

"Lady Kohdad?" Wake looked over to the girl he had bumped to the floor. "I'm really sorry. I didn't see you."

She was a beautiful girl, but she wasn't exactly what came to mind when Wake thought of a lady. He pictured someone in dresses, gloves, and fancy hats. Lady Kohdad looked more like she was ready to start a fight or show up to some kind of royal dance battle.

"Zessa, that's enough." The girl dusted off her long furry boots. "Do you not know an accident when you see one?"

The others came out and helped Wake to his feet as the human-like Zessa pulled his spear back. "Yes, ma'am. Sorry, ma'am."

"So much for not being seen." Twig elbowed Wake.

"Doesn't count," Wake whispered back. "We aren't even in the castle yet."

"Oh, my—" He rubbed his face. "I guess it could have been worse."

"I'm sorry about them." Lady Kohdad set her sights on Wake and inched her way over. She looked as human as either of the boys, and she looked to be around the same age as Wake, just like Twig. "My personal guards can be—a lot." She held a hand out. "I am Lady Kohdad. Who are you? You don't look like the kind of people who'd be headed to a party like this."

He took her hand. "I—I'm Wake." The sweet scent of her perfume flustered him. "This—this is my brother Desi—and this is Aza and Twig."

She stepped back and gave him a smile that could have emptied the thoughts of anyone. "Nice to meet you all. Would you be interested in accompanying me to the castle?" She gestured to a large carriage being pulled by two giraffe-necked horses. "I prefer to walk, but I'd be happy to give you all a ride."

"Lady Kohdad, we can't take these commoners with us. I can smell it—those boys must be normal humans. There's no way they were invited to the—"

She held up her hand and Zessa stopped. "They do appear to be ordinary humans." She narrowed her eyes. "What business does your group have at the castle?"

Wake looked to the others for any kind of help. He had no idea what he was supposed to say. Thankfully, Twig stepped forward. "You'll be delighted to hear that we're interested in ruining the Hog King's day."

Desi started to sweat. "Twig, what are you—"

"It's okay." He turned to Lady Kohdad. "That is something that would please you, is it not?"

She studied the group, her eyes falling on Wake again. "Is that true?"

Twig spoke first. "As true as—"

She held a finger up. "I want to hear from him." Her finger pointed right at Wake.

Wake could feel his heart beating even faster.

"Uh—yeah. What Twig said is true." He looked over at Desi. "My brother and I, we got stuck here. We've been sent out to get a couple of artifacts from the islands so we can go home. Apparently, the Hog King has one of them or something."

"You are humans then."

"That's what they tell us." He looked to see whatever it was that made her not quite human. It had to be something small like Twig's tails. "Are you—?"

"Human?" she asked. "No. Not entirely at least, but I'll let you wonder what it is that makes me different." She looked toward the castle. "If you want to steal from the Hog King, you're going to need a way to get through the guards by the gates."

"There's guards by the gates?" Desi asked.

"It only makes sense," Aza said as he looked toward Twig. "I just figured you had a plan."

He chuckled. "My plan was to wing it."

"We're going to end up behind bars by the end of the night."

Lady Kohdad clapped her hands. "Looks like you will need a ride after all." She started toward the carriage. "Come with me. We can get you past the guards, but after that, you're on your own."

"Wait a sec," Wake said. "Why would you help us?"

"Your fox-tailed friend there knows who I am. That means he knows the Hog King is nothing but a pain in my—backside." She opened one of the doors to the carriage. "If I can secretly be a part of ruining his day— his stupid party—honestly, just about anything of his— I'll take it."

Twig shrugged and they all followed her into the carriage. It felt strange that someone with such a luxurious carriage would have preferred walking. It was possible that Wake was biased, walking for days on end had left his feet covered with blisters.

She bumped the wall of the carriage and it pulled forward. "I understand what you humans are after," Her eyes fell on Twig and Aza. "But what about you and the Kola?"

Twig let out a nervous chuckle. "Can't a guy just be interested in helping two humans get home?"

"Not the likes of you."

Aza cleared its throat. "You aren't exactly subtle, Twig. I'm not with him. I'm keeping watch over the boys."

"Twig?" Lady Kohdad was waiting for some kind of answer.

He sighed. "I'm just after some of the Hog King's gold. You happy now?"

"I don't care why any of you are headed in there. All I require is honesty." She looked out one of the carriage's small windows. "Once we're past the guards, you'll only have a quick moment to hop out before we enter the castle walls and become surrounded by guards. Understood?"

"Well, how are we supposed to actually get inside?" Desi asked.

"You just leave that to me." Twig smirked.

"How long have you two been here?" She asked Desi with a warm smile.

"Just a couple of days, but—"

"But your family must be worried sick." Desi nodded and hung his head. She put a hand on his knee. "You boys will be home in no time. I bet your big brother is taking great care of you."

Aza scoffed. "More like, I am. These kids—" Lady Kohdad's glare shut it up.

"He is." Desi nodded.

Wake smiled and looked out across the glistening lake below. The water was so clear that it looked like the lake was a perfect copy of the night sky. What caught his attention were the small snowflakes that were falling all around.

"Is it—snowing?" Wake asked.

"That extravagant nut," Twig groaned. "The Hog King likes to have his castle's magic-man create snow for special events."

"But it's so warm out. How can there be snow?"

"Magic is a powerful thing."

Two thumps sounded and Lady Kohdad became serious. "Everyone be quiet. We are approaching the guards. We don't need Wake falling out of the cart and bumping into more people."

Wake rolled his eyes at her joke. "Alright."

Everyone held their breath as they listened to Lady Kohdad's group speaking with the castle guards. After a long moment, the cart pulled forward again without any trouble.

"It's time for you to sneak in," Lady Kohdad said. "I wish you all the best of luck."

"Thank you for all your help, ma'am." Aza reached for the door.

Everyone hopped out, but before Wake could, she grabbed his hand. "You two be safe, okay?"

Wake nodded. "Thank you, Lady Kohdad."

"Call me Leora."

There was something endearing about the way her name left her lips. There were a few girls at school Wake wouldn't dare to admit he had a crush on, but he had a feeling if Leora went to his school, every boy would openly drool over her.

"Thank you, Leora." Wake hopped out of the carriage and snuck toward the rest of the group.

They'd ducked behind a small section of the wall that extended out to the sides of the bridge. The guards were only a few steps away, but their boisterous oinking told Wake that they didn't have much to worry about.

"What do we do now?" Wake looked up to the top of the wall. "That's a pretty big climb."

"We just gotta get a little more help." Twig pulled out his instrument once again. "Watch this."

Aza jumped at him. "The guards will hear."

Twig caught Aza with a hand and placed it on his back. "Sh. It'll be fine."

He played what was a gorgeous, but incredibly high-pitched song. Wake kept an eye on the guards the entire time, but it looked like they might have just assumed the music was coming from inside the castle. Twig ended on a piercing whistle of a note and looked off into the distance.

"That was a nice song and all, but what did that even do?" Desi asked as he looked around. "Was it a magic song? Can we jump really high now?"

Twig chuckled as he watched Desi take a pitiful hop. "Wait for it."

Wake stared where Twig had fixed his eyes. From the dark, a group of large birds was headed right for them. When they reached the wall of the castle, they each hovered above the last, creating a living staircase.

"Come on." Twig waved as he stepped up onto the first bird. "Be careful. I wouldn't want to take a fall like that."

"You first, Desi," Wake said as he helped him onto the first bird.

Stepping out over the lake was a scary thought, but the birds didn't budge under any of their weight. The staircase of birds was long and it winded around to the back of the castle's wall. They each made their way to the top, and Twig and Desi each climbed over the top of the wall.

When Wake poked his head up, Twig gestured for him to get back down. He spotted two guards making their way toward them and ducked back down.

"What is it?" Aza whispered.

"Two guards."

Wake heard Twig's instrument again, and the bird at the bottom of the formation flew over the wall.

"Are they going to get caught?" Aza asked.

"Kinda hard to tell when I can't see them."

It crossed its arms. "I don't need that kind of sass."

"Sh!"

The heavy steps of the guards passed by overhead. "Can't believe we're stuck on wall duty again."

"Better than being stuck in the party."

"How's that?"

"Anyone who screws up in there is done for. There's no pressure here. What kind of psycho is gonna scale the walls?"

One of the pigs laughed. "Good point."

Their voices trailed off along with their footsteps and Wake leaned back over the wall again. He watched the snowflakes fall from above and melt into nothingness before they even hit the ground—not even a drop of water to speak of. To his surprise, Twig and Desi weren't anywhere to be found.

"Twig? Desi?"

Desi's head poked up from the other side of the walkway. "Coast is clear?"

Wake nodded and hopped over the wall with Aza. He pulled Desi up as Twig hopped onto the wall as well. The bird Twig had summoned was working as a little platform for the two of them. They were lucky no one from the castle grounds below bothered to look up.

"Thank you," Twig said to the bird. "Tell your friends that we owe you our lives."

It squawked and flew off. The other birds followed it and soon they were all alone on the wall of the Hog King's mighty castle.

"Where now?" Aza asked.

Wake looked around and spotted a ladder leading up above the main room of the castle. "What about that?"

Twig gave him a playful slap on the back. "You're a natural thief as well. We'll get up high and see what we're working with before we head inside."

The group crept their way up the ladder and found a window. They looked through the window to the packed party below. The party was—a complete mess.

There were creatures of all kinds, but the room was mostly filled with different pigs all of which were dressed fancier than the last. The different creatures with their strange clothes made up of even stranger colours made for what looked like colour-vomit. Things were only made worse thanks to the green outfits of the castle's servers.

Wake spotted Lady Kohdad as she left a group of pigs. For a moment, it looked like she looked right up at him.

Aza groaned. "I can't even imagine how bad that room smells."

"There." Twig pointed to a staircase on the far side of the room. "That should be our way down to the Hog King's treasury. If he has whatever this artifact is supposed to be, it'll be down there somewhere."

"Great." Wake looked around. "We just need to find a way in, sneak down the stairs, find the artifact, and get back out without getting caught."

"Doesn't sound all that bad." Twig chuckled and threw his arms around Wake and Desi. "So, who's ready to party?"

Chapter 13:
The Flurris Castle Heist

It took a while for the group to find an actual way into the castle, but eventually, they came to an open window leading to a smokey kitchen. Wake expected it would be filled with chaotic chefs all rushing back and forth, but there was just one cook with his back turned to the window.

"Where is everyone?" he asked.

"What? You think they're all gonna be cooking during the party?" Aza asked. "They probably spent the last week preparing for the party."

Twig nodded. "I bet that guys there in case there's any special requests." His expression changed as he reached through the window. "No way."

"Careful!" Desi said.

Twig held out a dark green dress shirt. "This looks an awful lot like the uniforms the servers in the party were wearing."

"Most of them looked like they were some kind of strange—"

"Some kind of strange creature? Monster? You were gonna use one of those words, right?"

Desi hung his head. "I didn't mean it like that."

"It doesn't matter." Twig grabbed a few more uniforms. "Everyone put these on. Aza, you can stick with me. If we all try to avoid drawing attention to ourselves we'll be fine."

"If you hadn't noticed, the boys are pretty bad at that." Aza chuckled.

Twig pulled the uniform on. "Most people won't bat an eye at a couple of servers if we look like we're already busy with something else." He hopped through the window and grabbed an empty tray.

Desi and Wake followed him into the kitchen. The slight scent that was wafting toward the open window hadn't done the delicious smell justice. As soon as they were within the smokey warmth of the kitchen, the sweet smell of barbecue and fresh vegetables filled Wake's nose.

They both grabbed empty trays as Twig ripped two other shirts apart. "What are you doing?"

"It's a bandana." He wrapped the piece of fabric around Wake's head and tied it. "The more of your features we hide, the less likely it is that someone will notice you're human."

"How many times have you done something like this?" Aza asked.

"Well—I suppose—" Twig started to tie the other piece of fabric around Desi's head. "You probably don't want to know the answer to that."

"What's the plan?" Wake asked as he adjusted his bandana.

"We all get out on the floor and spread out." Twig peered out the door to the party. "We need to get to that staircase we spotted, but we can't go as a group. That'll look way too suspicious."

"I don't know if I'm comfortable letting Desi go off on his own like that"

"We don't have much of a choice—"

"I can do it," Desi said.

Everyone stared at the determined young boy.

"Looks like he's spoken." Twig smirked.

Wake put a hand on his shoulder. "You sure?"

He nodded. "I'm sure."

Aza jumped from Twig's back to Desi's. "He's not alone. I'll keep an eye on him."

"Hey! What are you guys doing in here?" The lone cook must have heard all the commotion. "You're supposed to be on the floor. Don't come sneaking in here for a break. I ain't taking the fall for a bunch of lazy bums."

"Yes, sir!" Twig replied. "One of the new trainees had a bit of an accident. Needed to grab some more trays."

"Oh, my apologies." The cook turned back to whatever he was working on. "Good luck out there. I know I'd hate to be the trainee that screwed up."

"Let's get going before we get yelled at again," Wake said as he pushed the door open. "Get to the stairs. Regroup wherever we can down there."

Everyone walked out into the bustling party and fanned out through the crowd. Being down on the floor, it was clear that there weren't quite as many pigs as Wake had initially thought. The party was as diverse as any of the villages the boys had visited previously.

He watched as Desi and Aza disappeared toward a huge staircase that led further into the castle. "Aza will keep him safe—hopefully."

Wake figured his best bet to get toward the stairs would be if he looked like he was checking on the nearby table of food and drinks. The closer he got, the tastier the food looked. He wasn't sure what kind of drinks were available, because all of the many multi-coloured drinks resembled Desi's favourite sports drinks.

"Ugh. Now they're letting the help near the food?" a familiar female voice joked. "How low can this party go."

"Oh. I'm sorry. I'll just—"

"Wake, relax."

Wake turned around to see Lady Kohdad smiling at him. "Lady Kohdad."

"I told you, you can call me Leora."

"Leora, how'd you know it was me?"

"Don't worry about it." She snatched a small pastry from the table. "Want a taste?"

"I better not. Don't want to blow my cover."

"Your cover?" Leora popped the pastry into her mouth. "So serious."

He shrugged. "Seems like it could be pretty serious if we get caught."

"You aren't wrong."

"What are you doing? I figured someone as important-sounding as *Lady Kohdad* would be brushing shoulders with the fanciest people in here."

She looked around. "I did my rounds. The Hog King hasn't come down to the party yet apparently." She poked Wake's chest. "I wasn't planning on staying all that long, but I'm curious to see how you and your friends do."

"I'm glad my potentially life-or-death situation is fun for you."

"Oh, don't be so dramatic," she giggled. "Where are all your friends?"

"We thought it would be best to spread out. We're headed for the staircase over there." Wake stuck a thumb in the direction of the stairs.

"You mean that staircase currently being watched by a guard?"

He looked over to see Desi and Aza's heads sticking out from below. A guard had stopped in front of the entrance and was now watching the party-goers. Wake figured he had to be the last one to need to get downstairs. Twig probably headed straight for the stairs —he did have the most experience.

"Crap."

"Looks like you need my help yet again."

"What do you mean?"

She pulled out a tube of lipstick and rolled it on, turning her lips to a shade of deep purple. "What? You think I'm not pretty enough to act as a distraction?"

"Uh—well—I—you—"

She laughed and slapped his shoulder. "Relax. I'll go and keep the guard busy. I'll only do my best to entice him if I absolutely have to, but trust me, these pigs aren't that bright."

"Entice?" Wake followed close behind her. "The people here do seem—pretty into themselves."

"That's putting it lightly." She nodded. "The rich folk here are so self-absorbed, they'd try to sell you if they thought it would mean a better life for themselves."

"Are you rich?"

"I am," She looked back and winked. "But we aren't all bad."

Wake stopped off to the side as Leora headed toward the guard. "Excuse me, sir?"

The guard straightened up when he noticed who was getting his attention. "Lady Kohdad, it's a pleasure to see you back in the castle. Are you in need of something?"

"Not so much me." She shot Wake a cheeky look. "I've been told that there is some sort of trouble with the women's washroom. Someone's shut themselves inside and won't let anyone in—or something like that. Is there anything you could do about that?"

She wasn't the best liar, but the guard didn't look like he suspected anything.

"Well, I can't exactly leave my post. I just got here and I was already running late." The guard scratched his belly. "I can grab the next guard I see and see if they can solve the trouble for you."

Leora looked around the party. "I don't see a single guard around here, do you?"

"No, ma'am."

"Well then, considering I'm facing a bit of an emergency here, maybe you should see to it that the problem is dealt with." Leora crossed her legs a bit and raised an eyebrow. She pointed toward Wake. "I'll have him watch the staircase until you return—unless he's called away to tend to his duties, that is."

"I think I understand, ma'am." The guard looked from her to Wake and gave an understanding nod. "I'll go check right away. I shouldn't have given you any hassle. I'm so sorry."

She grabbed the guard as he rushed past. "Relax. I'm not going to report you to anyone."

"Oh," The guard looked like he was ready to cry. "Thank you—thank you, Lady Kohdad. I'll make sure that washroom is clear right now, and I'll run right back —just for you."

"Thank you—" she said, waiting for a name.

"Clyde."

"Thank you, Clyde."

Clyde nodded and rushed off into the party.

"Okay, you're way too good," Wake said as he rushed over.

"Yeah, what an idiot." She looked off to where the guard had disappeared. "I could have just sent my people to do something like that." She smiled at Wake. "But there you go. Go get that artifact."

"I owe you big time."

"You do." She ran a finger along Wake's arm. "But we can talk about that the next time I see you."

"So, I'll see you again?"

She kissed Wake on the cheek. "I'll find you at some point. I've got a nose for that sort of thing."

Wake smiled and gave her a nod before heading down the spiralling staircase. As he reached the bottom, a strong hand pulled him into a dark corner.

"What the heck took so long?" Twig asked in a hushed tone.

"Sorry. I got held up. A guard took his post up there before I could sneak down here."

"How'd you get past him?" Desi leaned closer. "Is that lipstick?"

"Don't worry about it." Wake rubbed his cheek where Leora had kissed him. "Were you guys just waiting down here the whole time or did you take a look around?"

"I get it." Twig grinned and nudged him with his elbow. "You bumped into Lady Kohdad again didn't you."

"What? No, I—"

Desi started laughing. "Oh! You two like each other, don't you?"

"Leora helped me get down here, that's all."

"Leora? Wake and Leora climbing through the—"

"Can we focus on the task at hand, please?"

"Young lover-boy is right," Aza said, which caused Wake to groan. "We need to get what we came for and get out of here."

"Right." Twig snapped right back to his serious expression. "I got down here first and took a bit of a look around. There are some patrols down here, but nothing we shouldn't be able to avoid." He pointed down a hall. "There's a room full of treasures over there. I figure if we're going to find your artifact, it'll be in there."

Aza hopped onto Twig's back. "Lead the way."

Twig nodded and headed down the hallway with Wake and Desi following close behind.

Desi tapped Wake's shoulder. "I told you I'd be okay on my own. I didn't even need Aza's help."

Wake screwed up Desi's hair. "You did good, buddy."

"I even beat you down here."

"You did. Maybe you should be taking care of me."

Desi looked like he was proud of himself. It may have been a small accomplishment that didn't matter at the end of the day, but Wake wasn't going to make him feel less special. Everyone deserved to feel like they got a win sometimes.

They came around the corner to a room filled with shimmering golden treasures. It looked like pretty much everything in the room cost more than their house back home.

"You two know what you're looking for?" Twig asked.

"Yeah, a strange orb," Wake said.

"Strange orb?" Twig looked around. "Alright, you two take a look around and see what you can find, but don't touch anything other than your orb." He looked over to a set of doors. "There's some patrols, and I'm still after the King's gold, so Aza and I will take a look through there."

Wake gestured to the treasures. "Gold. Right there."

Twig shook his head. "Gold coins go a lot further than weird idols."

"Okay." Wake nodded. "You guys be careful."

"Don't touch anything," Aza said as it wagged a claw. "Just the orb."

"We know Aza."

"Just drilling it into your heads."

"Go find that gold."

Twig and Aza disappeared behind the doors. Wake turned to Desi and smiled. "Let's find this artifact."

The boys crept through the room, looking at all the magnificent treasures held inside. Both of them were amazed by an entirely gold suit of armour. They scanned the entire room and finally came across the glowing orb on a lone pedestal.

"There it is!" Desi started toward it.

"Use your head." Wake grabbed his wrist and pulled him back. "See how it's separate from everything else? I bet there's some kind of trap."

"Really?"

Wake nodded. "It might be some kind of alarm—or maybe arrows will shoot out." He scratched his head. "It's kind of hard to guess what sorts of things we'll find on these islands."

"It doesn't look like there's any traps. Just looks like they put the orb somewhere else."

Footsteps down the hallways they had come from caught Wake's attention and he pulled Desi behind a high stack of treasures.

"What?" Desi whispered.

"Someone's coming."

The footsteps ran into the room. It was a patrol of pig guards.

"You're certain you aren't mistaken?" one of the guards asked.

"I'm sure. We're missing some staff uniforms. A server was supposed to watch the stairs for me while I took care of something, but when I got back, he was gone," Clyde said.

"Clyde," Wake groaned under his breath.

"Clyde? Who's—" Desi was cut off when his shoulder bumped a golden shield to the floor.

"Desi—" Wake whispered through gritted teeth.

"What was that?" one of the guards asked.

The footsteps came closer.

There was nowhere to go.

"What do we do?" Desi asked.

"We go to jail—probably—hopefully."

"Hopefully?"

Wake shrugged. "Jail is probably better than death."

"Whoever's there, come out now and we won't hurt you." Wake sighed and stepped out with Desi. "Who are you?"

"We're—"

"Those are the stolen uniforms," Clyde oinked.

"You're sure?"

"I'm sure."

Wake glanced toward the door Twig had gone through. He and Aza were staring in. It looked like they had no idea what to do.

Wake turned his attention back to the pigs. "We can talk about this. This is all one big misunderstanding."

"Misunderstanding, huh?"

"That's right."

The lead guard brought a hand to his face. "Men, take them to the dungeons."

There were times on the islands where things seemed bad, but for some reason, being a prisoner to a bunch of pigs felt like it was the worst of all.

Chapter 14:
One Large Cell

Wake never thought he'd find himself behind bars, but his short time spent on the island had already shown him that many of the things he previously believed were wrong.

He wasn't sure how long they'd been in the cell, but after seeing the sunrise, Wake knew things weren't going well. Twig and Aza had to be somewhere inside the castle still. Maybe they were looking for a set of keys or a way into the prison. The boys hadn't heard from or even seen either of them since they were jailed, but they had to come for them, right?

Desi's loud yawn pulled Wake from his thoughts. "You sleep okay?"

"Cold cell and a rickety piece of wood to lay on?" Desi blinked away the remainder of his slumber. "Nope."

Wake focused on the bars of the cell again. If Twig and Aza weren't going to be able to help them, then maybe he could figure out an escape route.

"Still nothing?" Desi asked.

"Nothing." Wake pulled on the bars, but they didn't budge. "No guards. No Aza. No Twig." Wake let go of the bars and sighed.

"There's gotta be a way out of here." Desi looked around, but his sight fell back on Wake and his tired eyes. "How much did you sleep?"

"Enough."

"Doesn't look like—"

"I'm fine."

"Okay, but—"

"Desi." Wake glared at him. "I'm fine."

Desi flipped open his bag. "At least they didn't take our things. Maybe one of us has something we could use to pick the lock or bend the bars."

"They didn't take our things because we aren't breaking out of here with food, napkins, and a weird key. Before you ask, no. The key doesn't fit the lock." Wake set his back to the wall and sunk to the floor. "Besides, even if we could pick the lock—I have no clue how to do something like that, do you?" Desi shook his head. "That's what I thought."

"Well, let's look on the bright side." Desi pulled a small piece of food from his bag. "At least we have some food."

"Don't you get it?" Wake smacked the piece of food out of his hand. "There is no bright side. The only reason we have our food is because those pigs are too lazy and too greedy to bother feeding us some of their food. That's it."

Desi looked shocked by Wake's outburst, but that shock morphed into anger. "You don't have to be so mean. I'm just trying to help."

Wake turned back to the bars of the cell and stared at the door. "You can help by keeping quiet. I'm trying to figure out what to do. It's your fault we're even in here." He brought a hand to his chin. "Maybe there's some way we could signal Twig and Aza."

He pictured throwing some of their belongings out the small cell window in an attempt to get the attention of—someone. The issue with that was that he had no idea where in the castle their cell was. For all Wake knew, the cell window could have faced out toward the lake.

"Won't work."

Wake's ears practically perked up when he heard footsteps coming from down the hall.

"What about—"

"Sh," Wake interrupted without turning around.

"Okay, I told you I'm only trying to—"

"Sh. Footsteps."

Desi's eyes went wide and he crept over to Wake. "Do you think it's someone coming for us?"

"I don't know."

"Maybe Aza and Twig found their way to us. That's totally possible right?"

"I don't know, Desi."

"I'd like to think that's the case."

"Don't set yourself up for disappointment. It's just as possible that they got caught, and those footsteps are them being dragged to another cell."

"Huh." Desi pushed his head against the bars with his ear jutting out. "No."

"No? What do you mean no?"

"I don't know about Twig, but Aza would be kicking and screaming the whole way."

Of everything Desi had said during their time on the island, nothing had sounded as correct as that.

"Good point, but let's keep their names quiet. As far as we know, they could still be in the castle and the pigs might not even know it."

"Good idea."

The footsteps pounded, closer and closer, until the boys were face to face with a handful of spear-gripping guards. None of them looked happy to be there, and their faces showed how taxing the multiple flights of stairs were.

"You guys should really exercise more," Wake laughed.

"Quiet—you—horrid—little human," the lead guard coughed and wheezed. "The—mighty Hog King —has—summoned you."

"What are we waiting for?" Wake crossed his arms. "Big strong guards should be ready to go, right?"

"My—men have—worked very hard—just a—five-minute break."

Desi laughed at them. "You guys should do that running test—the beeping one from my school."

"Running—test? Beeping? What are you talking about?" the guard asked.

"Never mind." Desi stifled another laugh.

Wake's eyes set on Clyde, the guard that had caught them. "Hate you, Clyde."

"What—did I—do?" he squealed between deep breaths.

"Wouldn't be here if it weren't for you," Wake said with a shrug.

"I'm not the one—that broke in. Not my fault."

"Doesn't mean I can't hate you."

"I guess that makes sense." Clyde accidentally knocked his spear against his head and brought a hand to where it had hit. "You humans sure are mean."

"We are?" Wake raised an eyebrow. "You're the one that threw us into jail without asking us any questions."

"Enough! All of you!" The lead guard straightened his posture. "It's time for your trial."

Wake and Desi gave each other a confused look. "Trial?"

The pigs weren't joking.

The boys were led down flight after flight of stairs, until they were back in the same room the party had been held in the night prior. Rather than the beautiful party fixtures, the room was now filled with everything

Wake had ever seen in those court drama shows his mom watched.

Wake couldn't help wondering what their sentence might be.

"You've gotta be kidding me," Wake said as the guards pushed him into the centre of the room.

There was a full gallery of well-dressed pigs that stared at the boys. It looked like the pigs were all offended by the sight of them.

"Why would—we be—kidding?" the lead guard said, once again out of breath.

"I thought you said the Hog King wanted to speak with us?"

"What do you think is about to—"

A loud blast of brassy horns rang out through the room. There were two pigs stood atop the great staircase that Wake had seen the previous night playing two strange instruments. They were big brass horns, almost like tubas, but they resembled bagpipes more than any other instrument the boys had ever seen.

"Announcing the arrival of his royal majesty, the Hog King!" the pigs squealed.

Desi nudged Wake. "What's the difference between a pig and a hog?"

"I dunno." Wake cocked his head. "Maybe a hog is bigger than a pig? Could just be a dumb naming thing."

Clyde tapped Wake with his spear. "You'll watch your tongue when his majesty is being—"

"Shut up, Clyde," Wake snapped. "Still hate you. Don't wanna hear it."

"Oh."

The Hog King stepped into view, and whether or not a hog was bigger than a pig, this hog was huge. He was far bigger than any of the pigs that Wake could see by quite a bit. Being king must have meant that he had first dibs on whatever food they managed to get their hands on—and they must have had a lot of food.

The way the crowd murmured and oohed as the Hog King approached told the boys that the king held all the power. He wasn't just some symbol of an older era.

The Hog King reached the bottom of the stairs and took a deep breath. He'd already become covered in sweat. "I thought—I told you—to have those stairs—taken in!" the Hog King squealed at his guards.

"Your majesty, that's not possible."

He glared at the guards. "Make it possible."

"Yes, sir!"

The Hog King stepped behind a large platform and made his way into an even larger chair. He swapped out his intricate gold crown for one of those silly white-haired judge wigs. Of all the strange things this island did differently from home, of course, they'd decide to do that the exact same.

"Two humans broke into my castle during my party and attempted to steal some of my belongings. Is that correct?" The Hog King asked as he stared down at the boys.

"Yes, sir!" the guard repeated.

The Hog King held up a hand. "I was speaking to the humans."

"Sorry, Sir!"

He rolled his eyes. "Well?"

Wake leaned toward Desi's ear. "Let me do the talking." He nodded and Wake stepped forward. "This is all a really big misunderstanding. We—"

"A misunderstanding you say?"

Wake raised an eyebrow. "Yes?"

"This changes things." The Hog King scratched his fat belly. "A misunderstanding certainly does."

"It does?" the boys asked.

"Of course! We were just going to execute you—you know, sentence you to death. Quite the nasty thing." The Hog King banged a small gavel and chuckled. "But I suppose if it is a misunderstanding, as you say, then we must have a proper trial." He looked around the room. "Where is your representative?"

Wake looked around the pig-filled make-shift courtroom. "Representative?"

"Your lawyer."

Wake looked from Desi to the Hog King. "We don't have one."

"Then one shall be appointed to you." The Hog King raised a finger and pointed at Clyde.

"Wait, no. We don't want—"

"You there. What is your name?" the Hog King asked.

Clyde stepped forward, still clutching his spear. "Clyde, your majesty."

"Clyde?" The Hog King looked to a nearby guard. "Have a word with his parents. What kind of a name is Clyde?"

"Thank you, sir," Clyde said as his entire body trembled.

"You will represent these boys in their trial. Do you have any objections?"

Wake's hand shot up. "We do. We don't really want that—"

The Hog King raised a hand and spears pointed toward the boys. "I believe I was speaking with Clyde, young man."

Clyde opened his mouth like he had an objection, but the eyes of the gallery must have shocked him into keeping quiet.

"Nothing? Excellent! Clyde has been upgraded to court lawyer for the tiny humans." He banged his little gavel. "We'll have a quick break for food while Clyde speaks with the humans."

The room shot into a loud murmur as Clyde rushed toward the boys. "Looks like I'm your defence."

"How are you supposed to defend us if you're part of the reason we got caught in the first place?" Desi asked.

"You're kinda the worst, man," Wake said.

"I'll do my best to help you. You don't seem like bad people. I think I can talk him out of the death sentence."

"You think?" Desi asked.

"We'd be better off defending ourselves." Wake tapped a finger on the side of his head. "I saw how you reacted when everyone stared at you."

"The Hog King isn't going to listen to a pair of humans," Clyde squealed. "You're lucky that even went down the way it did. Life in jail is going to be better than whatever punishment the Hog King could come up with."

"You sure about that?" Wake asked.

Clyde nodded. "He looks mischievous today. That's never a good sign when it comes to creating punishments."

Wake sighed. "What's the defence plan?"

"I'll ignore the part where you snuck past me—"

"Because it makes you look bad."

"That's not why."

"That totally is why."

"Whatever. We'll go for the whole, you wandered in without knowing what's going on and found yourselves in the Hog King's treasure chambers. That's believable, right? Right? It's not like humans visit these islands too often."

Wake and Desi gave each other an unconvinced look before staring at Clyde. "You've never done this before, have you?"

"Not once."

Wake put a hand on Desi's shoulder. "We're doomed."

The sound of the gavel banging told Wake that the Hog King had eaten enough of a snack. "Are we ready to proceed?"

"Y-yes, your majesty," Clyde squealed.

"Come now." The Hog King pointed at his wig. "Get it right."

"My apologies, your majestic honour."

"Much, much better! Please, proceed with your defence, and remember, if it's not good enough to convince me, these boys' lives are in your hands."

The boys watched Clyde gulp. "I'll do my best." He approached the Hog King and took a shaky breath. "These human boys found themselves lost in our strange land—as we know many humans do. If you were lost in a strange land, where is the first place you would go?" The crowd murmured and the Hog King's eyes darted around. "Well, I'd go right to the biggest landmark I can see. A castle." The Hog King raised an eyebrow in interest, and Clyde capitalized on that interest. "A magnificent castle, home to a magnificent ruler."

"My—" the Hog King smiled. "Do go on."

Clyde cleared his throat, it looked like the nerves had worn off. "The boys head to your beautiful castle for the aid of the marvellous king. Who'd be better suited to help the helpless?"

"Certainly no one else," the Hog King chuckled.

"Precisely! The unfortunate matter was that the boys weren't used to such a tremendous party. Through the crowds of strange beings and mighty pigs, the boys found themselves turned around. They wandered down an unguarded staircase and found themselves in your treasure room—purely by accident."

Wake wasn't going to hold his breath, but Clyde had far surpassed his expectations. He made his way back to the boys and smiled.

The Hog King leaned forward and looked at the boys. "Is this true? Are these events accurate to what you experienced?"

The boys nodded. "Yes, your—majestic—honour."

"I am a just ruler." The Hog King sat back in his chair. Desi squeezed Wake's arm in delight, but Wake could sense that the king had more to say. "But the two of you were far too close to my treasures to simply walk out of this castle unpunished. The only question now is what should your punishment be?"

"I was going to thank you, but you suck, Clyde," Wake whispered.

"Yeah, I'm with Wake on this one," Desi said.

"Clyde!" the Hog King squealed. "Assemble five of the finest people in attendance today. They shall assist me in coming up with a suitable punishment for the boys."

Clyde nodded and headed toward the crowd of pigs. He looked back for a moment, but Wake's frustrated stare scared him right back into his task. He grabbed five pigs and they all headed over to the Hog King.

"What do we do now?" Desi whispered.

"I don't know." Wake looked from the big doors leading out of the castle to a couple of the large windows. "We could try to make a break for it."

"Think we could make it?"

"I don't think it's going to matter much either way."

Desi scratched his head. "What if the punishment they decide on isn't all that bad?"

"Listen to the words you just said. Punishment—not all that bad." Wake looked around the room.

There had to be some way for them to make it out of the castle. A tug on his arm came from Desi, but he didn't have enough time to bicker anymore. He needed to find an answer.

The relentless tugging finally got to Wake. "What?"

"Look." Desi stared at a set of stairs.

Wake followed his eyes until he spotted both Aza and Twig. They were hidden just behind a small turn in the wall, and luckily, the commotion in the room was keeping eyes off of them.

Wake wasn't sure what would happen next, but he knew that they had just found their way out.

Chapter 15:
An Explosive Trial

"Do you think they have a plan?" Desi asked.

"I don't know." Wake tugged Desi so he wouldn't look at them. "But if someone spots them because of us, it won't matter."

"What do we do then?"

He shrugged. "There's nothing we can do. We gotta wait for them to make a move. If things take a bad turn, just do as I say."

The Hog King returned to his seat and slammed his little hammer on it. "Attention!" The room fell silent and all eyes fell on the boys. "We have come to our decision on the most suitable punishment for the humans. Instead of being sentenced to death, they will be sentenced to eternal servitude to yours truly."

The room burst into a round of applause as Clyde made his way back over. "I tried. That's the best I can do."

"Shut it, Clyde." Wake glared at him. "Trying wasn't good enough."

"Why are you so mean to me?"

"Oh, I dunno, maybe it's because you're a huge disgusting pig that did nothing for us." Gasps rang out throughout the room and it became clear that everyone was listening. "All we want is to go home, and now we're stuck here because of you."

"I just—"

~ *sssssssssssssssssssssssssssss* ~

Wake didn't care who was listening. "No. You literally did nothing. You didn't help us in the slightest. Why don't you go run up a couple flights of stairs? Fitting punishment for a crappy lawyer."

~ *sssssssssssssssssssssssssssss* ~

"That is enough!" The Hog King snarled.

~ *sssssssssssssssssssssssssssss* ~

"Humans will not ever, ever, ever, EVER, speak to our kind like—like—"

~ *sssssssssssssssssssssssssssss* ~

"Okay, what in the world is that irritating noise?" The Hog King looked around.

~ *SSSSSSSSSSSSSSSSSSSSSSSSSSSSS* ~

Wake looked toward where Aza and Twig were out of the corner of his eye. He knew what that sound was. The room was about to get loud.

~ *SSSSSSSSSSSSSSSSSSSSSSSSSSSSS* ~

POOF — POOF — SCREEEECH! KABOOM! KABOOM! KABOOM!

"TAKE COVER, EVERYONE!" the Hog King shrieked. "GUARDS! PROTECT ME!"

Two huge puffs of smoke started to fill the room from where the boys were standing as a massive firework went off. The explosion seemed like it would never end as the people in the make-shift court ran for their lives.

Twig rushed over with Aza on his back and they grabbed the boys. "You guys okay?"

"Didn't want to just break us out of jail?" Wake asked as they rushed through the door toward the kitchen.

"Trust us, we tried," Aza said. "Those pigs may be lazy, but there's a lot of 'em."

They made their way through the kitchen and came face to face with a wave of guards who had thought to hide there after the commotion began.

"What are you—"

Twig shoved the boys. "Run!"

"After them!" one of the guards shouted.

Everyone sprinted back toward the chaos of the previous room. The firework had finally finished going off, but the large puffs of smoke lingered. It was possible to see through them, but it was enough to create some confusion.

Wake looked toward the entrance, but it was guarded by another wave of pigs. "Where the heck do we go now?"

Aza pointed up the huge staircase the Hog King had come down. "That's our only option."

Everyone rushed up the stairs, and when they reached the top, Wake looked back to see a small army of pig guards charging toward them.

"Are we going to be able to get out of here?" Desi asked.

"Relax." Wake scoffed. "They'll be winded before they get halfway up the stairs. We've got time."

"That so?" Twig smirked as he looked at a series of staircases. "Let's keep on heading up then."

Everyone continued up the staircases, but the plan didn't make sense to Wake. "Not that I'm upset you guys saved us, but shouldn't we be looking for a way *down* to get out?"

"What? You aren't wondering where we were all this time?" Aza asked with two handfuls of Twig's hair for stability.

They turned a corner and headed up another flight of stairs. "I am, but our escape seems like the thing to focus on right now."

"Let's just say—your girlfriend is a life-saver," Twig said through huffs.

"Girlfriend?"

They made it up another flight of stairs only for the shouting of the pig guards below to gain the attention of a group above. As they started up another flight, a group of guards rushed toward them from above, and even more from the hallway behind them.

Wake looked between the two groups that had them trapped. "You guys didn't happen to plan for this, did you?"

"Does it look like we did, kid?" Aza asked.

"What are we gonna do?" Desi asked in a shaky voice.

"I don't know," Twig said.

Wake knew there had to be a way out of there. They couldn't have freed them, only for them all to be caught moments later. If their initial crime hadn't gotten them a worse sentence, escaping and then being caught again would.

The guards crept toward the group from each side and Aza sighed. "Twig?"

"Yeah, buddy?"

"Throw me."

"Throw you?"

"Yes. At them."

"But you'll—"

"Yeah, yeah, yeah. I know. I know." He smiled at Wake and Desi. "You boys find your way home, alright?"

"Hold on, Aza. There's gotta be another way," Wake said as he realized what was about to happen.

"What's happening?" Desi asked.

"Tell Ms. Ebbie and Dub how much I love 'em and —and have some pie for me. Once they're down, rush past them and find another way out." It tugged at Twig's hair. "Do it."

Twig looked horrified, but all of them knew it was the only way. He took Aza by his armpits and tossed him down toward the wave of guards, knocking them down like a bunch of dominoes. He hopped right up at the ones he hadn't knocked over and pushed back at them. "GO!"

Twig dragged Wake and Desi down the stairs and through the empty hallways of the castle. Wake got one final look at Aza as he jumped toward more of the guards. The deeper they made it through the halls, the quieter the commotion became.

"I can't believe we just left him," Desi sobbed.

"We can all cry for him later, but right now we need to find a way out." Twig pulled the boys along. "He wouldn't want to make a sacrifice like that for us, only for us to get caught again."

They all passed an open room, but a large window caught Wake's eye. "Wait a sec." He doubled back, and sure enough, the window was wide open. "Will that work for an escape?"

Twig rushed toward it. "It's going to have to." He leaned out before sliding through it completely.

Wake leaned closer. "Where did he—"

Twig popped back into view, scaring both the boys. "What are you guys waiting for? Come on."

The boys looked out to see that there was a small platform outside the window. The boys stepped through and onto the platform, but there wasn't anywhere else for them to go.

"I'm gonna be honest with you, this escape plan sucks," Wake said as he looked down at what would be an enormous fall to the lake below.

"You aren't wrong," Twig said as he looked down. "But that's about to change."

"How's that?" Desi asked on shaky legs.

Twig had a mischievous look on his face. "How do you guys feel about heights, again?"

"Hate them," Desi said.

"That's unfortunate considering we're going to jump into the lake."

"Hold up." Wake took another look toward the lake. "If we do that from this high up, we're just going to splat against the water. That's like, science one-oh-one." Twig pulled his instrument out again and played a low beautiful tune. "Great song. Not exactly the time, unless you can summon a swarm of birds to carry us."

Twig rolled his eyes. "Have I steered you wrong so far?"

Wake and Desi narrowed their eyes at each other. "Not technically?"

"Then just trust me." He took a breath and grabbed them by the hand. "On three, we jump."

"I already hate it," Wake said.

"Me too," Desi agreed.

"They're out on the walls!" a guard shouted. "Get them!"

"Not much choice now," Twig said.

Wake looked out across the island. It was a gorgeous sight if it weren't for the impending drop. Something that caught Wake's attention was a small caravan set up on the shore of the lake.

"Three."

Wake felt Twig's grip tighten.

"Two.

Whatever Twig's song had or would do, needed to happen sooner rather than later.

"ONE!"

Twig pulled the boys off the side of the castle and they fell toward the lake below.

"Is this one of those *wait-for-it* moments?" Wake called.

A huge snake-like creature shot out of the lake and they landed on its head. It was the biggest creature either of the boys had ever seen, which made Wake wonder about just how deep the lake surrounding the castle was.

Twig ran a hand along the creature's scaled head. "Thank you, friend." He pointed toward the caravan. "Could you set us there?"

The creature shifted its long, slender body until its tail was lying near the edge of the lakeshore.

Wake tilted his head. "It wants us to slide——"

Twig pulled the boys down the creature's back before he could even finish his sentence.

"AHHHHHH!" the boys shrieked as they flew down the creature's body.

Wake had been snowboarding once in his life, and it was the perfect practice for sliding down a giant sea-serpent's back. As they reached the bottom of its long body, they each shot through the air toward the shore. As if by magic, big fish hopped out of the lake and acted as small steps until they reached solid ground.

Wake realized just how nerve-wracking the whole experience had been when his legs refused to let him stand any longer. "Never—again."

"Oh, come on!" Twig chuckled. "That was awesome!"

"You made it!" a familiar female voice said as multiple footsteps approached.

Wake looked up to see Leora with Zessa right behind her. "You *did* help them out."

She smiled. "We did what we could to help. Where is your Kola friend?" Everyone hung their heads. "Ah. My apologies. He was a good friend."

"Shall we be off, Lady Kohdad?" Zessa asked.

"Yes." She looked toward the castle. "We should leave as soon as possible. It is likely the Hog King will send his men after us." She turned back to Desi and Wake. "You two are headed toward Mulos, correct?"

"Yeah, we are." Desi still looked like he was in a daze, but Wake helped him to his feet.

"What about Aza?" Desi cried.

"We can always come back for the Flurris artifact later and try to help Aza then. I have a feeling that security is going to be set to max for the next little while."

"We can't just leave him."

Wake pulled Desi into his chest. "I know, buddy. We'll come back and help him before we head home. I promise."

"Lady Kohdad—" Zessa began

"Have a heart, Zessa!" She glared at him. "Go. Leave us, and make the preparations to head toward Mulos."

"Yes, ma'am." Zessa glared at Wake. It looked like he knew he screwed up as he headed toward the rest of the caravan.

She coughed as she made her way to the boys. "When you return for your friend, you will have all of my men and supplies at your disposal."

Desi looked up at her through puffy, red eyes. "Really?"

"Really," Leora said before launching into a violent coughing fit.

"You alright?" Wake asked.

"A little ill. Nothing to worry about, but like I already said, we really must be going." She looked toward Twig. "Are you planning on coming along?"

Twig looked like he wanted to head right back into the castle, but whether it was for Aza or for the gold he never got was a completely different question. "Yeah, Wake's right. That place is going to be on high alert. Best to lay low on the edge of the island."

"Then come." Leora took the boys by the hand and led them toward the caravan. "I expect the both of you to tell me all about your brave little Kola friend on the ride."

Chapter 16:
No Treasure is Good Treasure

Some time had passed—more time than the boys were comfortable with. Leora had her caravan pick up the pace toward the crossing between Flurris and Mulos. They'd cut it close—if they even made it at all. The idea of spending another minute in the land of the Hog King made the boys sick to their stomachs.

Being stuck on the island might not have been such a bad thing. Wake wanted to get home as soon as possible, for his mom and for Desi, but he knew it wouldn't be right to just leave Aza.

No matter what happened, Wake and Desi were going to go back for Aza.

"All of that—all of that was for nothing," Wake said through gritted teeth.

"And we lost Aza," Desi stifled a sob. "What do we do now?"

Wake watched as Desi's eyes filled with tears again. His hazel eyes blended with his teardrops in a way that if you couldn't see the redness of his face, it could have been hard to tell he was crying.

"You guys will be okay," Twig said. "I know people, and I can feel that more than I've ever felt most other things. You two will get everything you need in no time."

"Yeah, except we didn't even get the artifact." Wake bashed the side of the carriage. "Nothing but wasted time and a missing friend."

"Wake, don't talk like that," Leora said.

"Oh, I almost completely forgot about that—" Twig reached into his bag and pulled out the same glowing orb the boys had found in the Hog Kings treasury. "This is what you guys were after right?"

"That's it!" Desi perked up.

"How'd you get that?" Wake asked.

Twig spun the orb in his hand. "When Aza and I snuck back in, we figured our escape plan would go a bit smoother if we already had the artifact in hand. No sense in trying to go back for it if the castle was going to be waiting for someone to try to steal it."

"That's why you guys were hiding in that stairway?"

"Exactly, but I wouldn't use the word hiding. Stealthily waiting for the right moment is what I'd prefer." Twig handed him the orb. "So chin up. You guys aren't leaving the island totally empty-handed."

"All we had to do was sacrifice a friend." Wake took the orb and shoved it into his bag. He didn't even want to look at it. "We're just a couple of losers. I don't know how we're going to—"

"That's enough," Leora commanded. "Do you think Aza would want you moaning over him after what he did? I bet he'd be here yelling at you for dwelling on the very choice he made."

"I didn't—Lady—" He caught himself before what he assumed would only extend his earful. "Leora." Wake met her gaze, and her determined look gave him new strength.

"Your friend did what he did because he believed so much that the two of you could make it home on your own, otherwise he never would have done it." She leaned back and looked out the small window of the carriage.

"Sacrificing himself, and trusting that you two don't need him anymore? That sounds like the biggest compliment possible to me."

Wake looked over at Desi. Even he was in awe of her words.

"She's way better with her words than I am," Twig nudged Wake. "But yeah, I second that."

"Thank you, Leora," Wake said with a smile.

"Good. You're much more handsome when you smile." Her words managed to drive all the air out of Wake's chest for some reason. "Moping doesn't do anyone any favours."

"You didn't get any gold, though," Desi said, looking around for any piles of money.

"No, I didn't, but there's always tomorrow." Twig pulled a small coin from out of nowhere and twirled it between his knuckles. "New chances, new rich people. I'll get myself something nice soon."

Leora stared at him. "Don't go getting any ideas."

He smirked. "Don't worry a hair on that pretty, feral head. I don't make it a habit to steal from my friends." Twig looked out the window. "You guys are on your way to Mulos, right?"

Wake nodded. "But all we know is that there might be some danger on the island. Not much of a shocker at this point."

"I guess here's as good a spot as any for me to hop out." Twig chuckled.

"You aren't interested in coming with?" Wake asked. "I'm sure there's plenty of people to rob there. We're headed to Voxal after that too."

"Voxal isn't really my speed. It's a little too— destructive—for my tastes. Maybe one day I'll give it a visit, once it's cleaned up and someone who actually cares about the islands is running things."

Twig put a hand on the door, but Wake grabbed it first. "Can I ask something—before you go?"

Twig settled back into his seat with a shrug. "Shoot."

"It feels like everyone hates Voxal—or at least the way it's been run by Conah. Why hasn't anyone stopped it?"

"Stopped it? What do you mean?"

"Like, couldn't all of the islands band together and overthrow Conah? Then you guys could put a stop to whatever it is that's making all that smog and protect all the islands."

"If only it were a perfect world," Leora said with a frown.

"Yeah—" Twig rubbed the back of his head. "Things are a bit more complicated than that. It's hard to get the islands to agree on anything. Could you imagine the Hog King sitting down with the likes of someone like—Amphinara—you met her right? That just wouldn't go well."

"But you don't think everyone would put their differences aside for the greater good?" Wake asked.

"No, I don't. The truth is, as much as everyone complains about Voxal, it's essentially a necessary evil. Most of the islands wouldn't be thriving the way they are without Voxal innovations—even just minor innovations. Everyone complains about it, but no one really wants to be the first to suffer the consequences of cutting that tie."

"So, people are afraid to make a change because it might make their way of life harder?"

"That does seem to be the case, but that's just the opinion of one foxy human." Twig banged on the carriage wall and it rolled to a stop. "It's time for me to head out. This journey is yours—I hope that's okay. I don't want you two thinking we aren't friends, because we absolutely are. I just—I think I want to stick with

Flurris for a while." He opened the door and hopped out. "I'll even see what I can do about Aza for you guys."

"Twig! Wait!" Desi called out as he rushed to the door of the carriage.

"What's up, little human?"

Desi pulled him close and hugged him. "Thank you for being a friend."

"You guys sure are affectionate, huh? Maybe humans aren't all that bad after all." Twig hugged him back and Wake watched a smile crawl across his face. "You take good care of your big brother, alright?" He let go and stepped back. "Make sure he's not bumping into any more women—or do, it looks like the last time turned out pretty good for him."

"Take care, Twig." Wake waved.

"Get home safe, Wake."

They shut the door and they were back on their way. Desi sat back down motionless, which worried Wake. It was understandable. The past few days had been quite the experience. The whole adventure was a lot for Wake, so it had to be even harder for Desi.

He put an arm around his brother. "He's going to be okay. We're going to be okay. Aza's going to be okay. Got it?"

Desi looked up at him with tears in his eyes again. "Got it."

"Good." The island started shaking, and Wake knew there wasn't much time left. "How far are we from the crossing?"

"It's going to be close," Leora said. "Zessa! Get a move on! As quick as we can go!"

It felt like the carriage doubled in speed the rest of the journey. Another crossing and another close call. There wasn't even time for Leora and her people to let the boys out. They were all trapped on Mulos for the time being.

"Welcome to Mulos," Leora said.

"I'm sorry." Wake winced as the islands shook and pulled apart once more.

"Sorry? What for?"

"Well you took us here, but now you're stuck here for now too."

She stuck her nose in the air. "And what makes you think we took you here? Maybe you just happened to be on board while my party travelled to Mulos." She ended with a wink.

"Really?"

"Really, really." She banged on the wall of the carriage and it came to a stop. "We have some business here for the next few days, so it's not a big deal at all. With that said, we'll leave you here to seek out your artifact."

"Wouldn't going together be a better idea?"

"Where we're headed, they don't exactly—*deal*—with humans. I'll keep an eye out for any strange artifacts for you, though."

"I understand." Wake nodded and hopped out of the carriage with Desi. "If you want to meet up again, our plan is going to be—head to the crossing between Mulos and Mahlurma for when the islands connect to Voxal—snatch the artifact from Voxal as quick as possible—head back to Mahlurma and get a group ready to get Aza back. Bing-bang-boom. We head home."

Leora giggled. "Well, I'm glad you've thought things out." She pulled a small object from her bag and handed it to Wake. "This is for you."

"What is it?" Wake studied it. "It looks like a firework."

"Sort of. It's just in case you two get into any trouble while you're on the island. I have a feeling you'll need it."

"How does it work?" Desi asked as he took a look at it.

"You point the end with the hole toward the sky and spin that bottom part." She tilted his wrist and ran a finger along the top of the strange object. "Just make sure your face isn't anywhere near it and that nothing's covering the hole."

"Kind of like a homing beacon?" Wake asked.

"Or like a screaming siren. We'll know the two of you are in trouble and my people will come as quick as we can, which shouldn't be too bad since this is the smallest of the islands."

Wake put it in his bag, and the boys stepped back from the large carriage. "I'm sure we'll see you again when everything goes to hell and we need some saving."

Desi nudged him. "Mum would kill you for swearing."

Wake stared down at him. "Do you really think that matters right now?"

The cart started moving again, but Leora stuck her head out of the carriage and waved as she laughed. "Yes, Wake. I'm sure that's exactly what will happen. See ya when you need some saving."

After a few moments, Wake and Desi were completely alone again.

Wake put a hand on his shoulder. "You ready for Mulos?"

Desi nodded. "We can do anything."

"You got that right."

Wake felt confident, but a wave of uneasy energy washed over him. It was the first island they'd have to explore on their own, and it wasn't even going to be the worst of the islands. He turned and stared at the island of Voxal—an island they were fast approaching.

Chapter 17:
The Village of Paradise

Mulos really was a lot smaller than the rest of the islands. The boys climbed their way to the top of the tallest hill they could find and found that they were able to see the entirety of the island. They could even see Leora's caravan rolling up to a small village.

Desi blocked the sun from his eyes. "Where do you think we should look first?"

"Good question." Wake peered around at the different villages. "It might be good for us to avoid the bigger villages now that we don't have Aza with us."

"Do you think there's more mean whale-people here?"

"Who knows." Wake chuckled. "Pretty hard to guess what we might find." He pointed toward a small cluster of huts near the island's edge. "Let's start there. It looks quiet enough."

Desi nodded. "I wish Aza was here. He'd know where to go."

"He'd act like he knew where to go while winging it just like everyone else," Wake said as he and Desi headed toward the village.

"No way. Aza was a great guide."

"*Is*—not was."

"Sorry." Desi stared at the ground.

Wake knew he'd been too forceful, but being forced to spend so much quality time with his little brother had become a bit much. There's only so long a teenager like Wake could spend with a kid like Desi before it really got annoying. Patience was never his strong suit.

"Don't apologize. We just—we don't need to talk about him like he's gone. We don't know what happened to him." Wake nudged Desi with his elbow. "Who knows? Aza is the kind of koala that might actually talk his way out of whatever trouble he got in."

"Kola."

Wake became annoyed all over again. "Alright, forget I said anything." He looked down toward the group of huts again. "Won't be long before we make it. Keep your eyes open for—anything."

The wildlife of Mulos was stranger than all the other islands. That was something Wake kept thinking as they explored each new island. Somehow, things kept getting weirder and weirder.

There were birds everywhere, but of course, there was a slight difference from the normal world. All the birds were covered in scales rather than feathers. It gave them a strange stuffed animal quality.

As they approached the huts, Wake became nervous since they were yet to see anyone on the island. The village itself was beautiful. The small huts had the perfect amount of tree coverage to provide shade, while still having plenty of places to soak in the setting sun. It was the kind of place Wake pictured whenever he heard people talking about retirement.

"Hello?" Wake called. "Is anyone home? Me and my brother could use a little help."

Desi grabbed his arm. "Should we be getting anyone's attention before we even know what these people are like?"

"We don't have a lot of time."

"Hello?" a female voice came from the inside of the hut nearest to them. "Someone there?"

"Hi, yeah. I don't want to alarm you or anything, but we're two humans that got lost here, so if you plan on eating us or throwing us in jail, could you just give us a five-minute head start?"

An ordinary woman stepped into view with a toothy grin. "We definitely aren't going to eat you guys. Been a while since any other humans have made it here."

"You're human?" Desi asked.

"Last time I checked—" She looked herself over. "Yep. Pretty sure I'm human." She took a step toward the boys, and they took a step back. "I guess you two being cautious makes sense." The woman crouched down and examined Desi. "My name's Gwyn. My grandma, Sylia, is inside. How'd you like to come and meet her?"

Desi stepped forward, but Wake grabbed his arm. "I'm not so sure about that one. We're looking for this island's artifact, so we can get home. You know anything about that?"

Gwyn shook her head. "I don't, but my grandma might. We were about to have some supper and there's plenty to go around. Are you two hungry?"

The truth was, the boys had eaten the last of their food on the way over to the island. Wake had no idea what plants might be poisonous or even if any of the animals were safe to eat—if he were even able to catch something. They were going to have to fill up on whatever they could, whenever they could.

Desi put a hand on his stomach, probably still hungry from the small meal they'd had earlier. "Wake?"

"I—I guess it couldn't hurt."

"Great!" Gwyn clapped her hands. "Come on then, just this hut here." She disappeared back inside the hut. Wake wasn't sure what it was, but something felt—off.

141

"We need to be careful here."

"They're human." Desi jutted a hand out. "How bad could they be?"

"What did I tell you about saying things like that?"

"Don't?"

Wake gave Desi a light push toward the hut. "Let's go see what's going on with these two."

When they walked into the hut the smell of fresh stew wafted toward them. Somehow it mixed with the salty smell of the nearby sea, which created the perfect combination of a savoury-salty scent. Wake could feel his mouth watering and his stomach grumbling, and he figured Desi was feeling the same.

The weird thing was there was no one around.

"Where'd that girl go?" Desi asked.

"I don't know." Wake pushed Desi behind him. "Be ready for anything."

Gwyn came around a small wall in the hut with a couple of wooden bowls in hand. "You two ready for some grub?"

Wake looked around the beautiful hut. "Where's your grandmother?"

"She was just laying down before supper. She's getting up there in age, so she needs little breaks when she can get 'em." She turned back to where she'd come from. "Grandma Sylia, you coming? The stew's perfect."

"Yes, yes, dear. I'm coming," a frail, scratchy voice said.

The boys weren't sure what to expect. It was possible that Gwyn was some creature in disguise setting a twisted trap. Sylia could have been a horrifying human-sized chipmunk that was interested in eating little humans for supper. Those ideas would have been crazy anywhere else, but not amongst the travelling islands.

When Sylia shuffled into the room, all of their worries washed away. She was any frail old woman they'd seen a thousand times. Her hair was a perfect sphere of a bun on the top of her head.

"You weren't kidding," Sylia said as she adjusted her crude glasses. "There really are other humans."

"Why would I have been lying? This hear is—" She looked over at the boys and cocked her head. "Well, I guess I never really caught your names, did I?"

"I'm Wake, and this is Desi."

"Wake and Desi." Sylia smiled. "Lovely names. What brings you two to our little corner of Mulos?"

"They're looking for some kind of artifact," Gwyn said as she poured stew into each of the bowls. "You wouldn't happen to know anything about that, would you?" She handed each of the boys a bowl of stew.

Sylia took a bowl from Gwyn and inhaled a steamy wisp from the stew. "An artifact, you say? Hmm." She brought a spoon to her lips. "I have heard whispers of an artifact here on the island, though I don't know where it is."

"Dang." Wake stirred his stew, waiting for either Sylia or Gwyn to try some first.

"At least we met some nice people this time," Desi said as he stared at his stew.

"We met nice people last time."

"And an army of pigs."

"Ah. You must have come from Flurris." Gwyn popped a spoonful of stew into her mouth. She raised an eyebrow at the boys. "Stew's gonna get cold if you two just keep staring at it."

Sylia did the same. "Yes. Let's continue this after supper, shall we?"

The boys nodded and dug into their stew as well. It was a wonderful combination of melt-in-your-mouth meat and fresh root vegetables. They were a little embarrassed by how fast they finished their helpings, but the women didn't seem bothered at all.

Gwyn looked out the window. "Ooh! Grandma, it's happening. Can we go outside?"

It had already become dark out, but the boys had hardly noticed. There was a strange blue-green glow approaching from the distance.

"Of course, child." Sylia turned to the boys. "Would you two like to see something incredible?"

"It's not dangerous is it?" Desi asked.

He could be annoying at times, but Wake was proud that Desi was learning to ask the right questions when it counted.

Sylia laughed. "We've never experienced any danger before." She shuffled toward the door. "Come. Come."

They followed the women out to the edge of the island and stared at the strange glow that floated toward them.

"What is it?" Wake asked.

"Just you wait." Gwyn said as she dangled her legs off the edge of the island. "Want to sit?"

"We're fine where we are."

"Gwyn?" Sylia said. "Tomorrow, will you pay all the village's quick little visits? You can ask them about the artifact the boys are seeking." She smiled at the boys. "They look like they could use a day to rest."

Gwyn smiled. "Of course. No trouble at all."

"You don't need to do that. We can find it," Wake said.

"We've been doing great so far," Desi added.

"I'm sure you boys have," Sylia said. "But there's no shame in a short break for your journey. I can make you boys up some meals for the remainder of your travels, while you rest and enjoy the sun. If you decide you absolutely must seek it out as well, then you can visit the villages as well."

Wake knew he could use the break, so he assumed the same was true for Desi. Both of their feet had to be pounding, and Wake's legs were about as stable as a bowl of fresh jelly.

"Alright, but if whoever has the artifact wants you to do something for it, you have to come get us." Wake looked back toward the glow as it neared. "It's not right to make you go through something like that for us."

"Then it's a deal. Gwyn said as a glowing jellyfish floated overhead. "They're here!"

Wake and Desi stared in amazement as the blue-green glow washed across the sky. It was a huge wave of jellyfish all floating just slightly above them. Wake wanted to reach out and touch one, but he remembered that a jellyfish's sting can be poisonous.

"It's beautiful," Wake said.

"Yeah," Gwyn smiled. "It's alright."

"The two of you can take the hut on the edge of the village. We have it set up for any travellers that come by." Sylia put a hand on each of the boy's shoulders. "Welcome to your stay in the village of paradise."

Chapter 18:
Hungry Hungry Harpies

Gwyn and Sylia were nice enough, but that didn't mean Wake was going to drop his guard. When the boys settled into their cozy hut for the night, he made sure to set a large pot on the edge of a chair right by the door. If someone tried to get in, it would fling to the floor, waking them both up.

When they woke up, nothing had moved. It put Wake at ease, but he couldn't shake a strange feeling in his gut. The boys weren't sure how long they slept for, but when they headed back outside, the sun was already high in the sky.

"Gwyn? Sylia?" Wake called as the boys approached the hut.

"That you boys?" Sylia said as she shuffled out of her hut. "Here I was, thinking the two of you were going to be sleeping all day."

"We've got a tight schedule," Desi said.

"Yeah, I think our bodies are trying to keep us on track," Wake said. "Where's Gwyn?"

"You don't remember what we spoke of last night?" Sylia sat down on a small rocking chair. "She's already set out to speak with the other villages. She'll probably be back soon."

"That's pretty quick." Wake raised an eyebrow.

He thought back to the sight from the top of the hill. The island was small, but the villages were spread out. The sun was high, but it didn't even look like it was noon yet. There was no way someone could have already been on their way back without sprinting from village to village.

"She left at first light. She's made the journey many, many times. She's the only human I've known to be welcome amongst the other villages." Sylia jutted a thumb toward her hut. "I already put together some meals for you boys. You're welcome to do whatever you'd like while we await her return."

Wake looked at the other huts in the village. "Where is everyone else?"

"Everyone else?" Sylia looked at the other huts like she forgot they even existed. "There is no one else, child."

"Then why are there all the other huts?" Desi asked. "You and Gwyn couldn't have made them all."

She laughed. "Quite right. This village was abandoned when we arrived years and years ago. We hoped someone—anyone—*anything* would come back eventually, but nothing ever did. We've just done what we can to be hospitable to anyone who travels this far."

"I guess that makes sense," Desi said.

Desi may have been convinced, but something wasn't adding up for Wake.

"We're going to go pack those meals into our bags," Wake said as he approached the hut. "You don't mind if we have something to eat now, do you?"

"Of course not. Help yourselves to anything you find."

"Awesome!" Desi said with a smile.

They walked into the hut, and Wake shut the door behind them. Desi gave him a confused look. "What are you—"

Wake clamped a hand over his mouth. "Quiet." He looked out the window, but Sylia hadn't moved. He pulled Desi deeper into the hut and pointed to an open window. "Something isn't right, and I need your help to see if I'm just being a paranoid psycho or not."

Desi pushed his hand. "What are you talking about?"

"I can't shake this feeling—like we're in danger here."

"Danger? Sylia and Gwyn are as nice as Ebbie and Dub."

"Yeah, maybe a little too nice, though. Look, all I need you to do is sneak over to one of the other huts and look around. If they all look like no one's lived there for a while, come straight back, but don't freak out if you see anything weird."

"You sound kinda crazy." Wake slugged his shoulder. "Ow!"

"Listen to your big brother."

"Why do I always have to do what you say?"

Wake slugged him again. "Because I'm older."

"Fine! You better apologize when I find nothing weird." Desi crawled through the window and crept toward the nearest hut.

Desi's anger toward Wake didn't matter. He needed to know if his feeling was real. Wake started snooping through the hut. All he needed was for one thing to be out of the ordinary. That's all he'd need to convince him to leave.

The problem was, the hut was just an ordinary hut. Gwyn and Sylia seemed to enjoy feather art as many of the huts' fixtures were covered with them. It was strange considering the birds on the island had scales instead of feathers, but he figured it couldn't have been hard for them to get feathers from another village or island.

Wake couldn't freak out over some weird decorating choices.

He searched through all the rickety drawers he could see, and even checked the small fridge. There weren't any signs of human meat, which was a good sign, but there wasn't much of anything. He turned his attention to the cupboards, but only found crudely fashioned bowls and cups.

That is, until he opened the cupboard that housed the women's plates. Right on top of the stack was a glowing plate—the same glow as the other artifacts.

He took it in his hands and stared at it. "If the artifact is here, what did Gwyn go to look for?"

Wake had so many questions.

Did Gwyn know the artifact was there all along?

Why did Sylia say that they didn't have it?

What was going on?

Wake was right.

There was something strange about the village.

He tossed the plate into his bag when he heard the creaking of the door. "Boys? It got pretty quiet in here, so I wanted to check if you're alright."

Wake rushed toward the entrance and came face to face with the old woman. "Sylia? Uh—everything's okay. We were—uh—we'd gone a while without a real meal, so we got pretty into the food."

She leaned to the side and looked toward the table. "You haven't touched the meals I made for you boys."

Wake took a quick look back. "Yeah—we figured we'd save those for when we left. We aren't really sure how much longer our journey will be. If we mess up, we could end up stuck on Voxal for six months or something like that."

"It is important to be careful, child. Many people get lost on Voxal and never return." She leaned again. "Where's your brother?"

"Desi? Oh, he must just be looking around. You two keep a beautiful home."

"Desi? Come out now, child."

"Grandma? What's going on?" Gwyn asked from outside.

Sylia whirled around. "Gwyn, you're back so soon. How was the trip?"

Wake took a deep breath and looked back into the hut in time to see Desi climb back into the hut with a horrified look on his face. There was no telling what he found in that hut.

"The trip was good. No one seemed to know anything about an artifact though."

Desi crept toward Wake and started rustling through his bag. Wake raised an eyebrow. "What are you doing?"

He pulled the small device Lady Kohdad had given Wake from the bag and stepped back. "Bones." Desi sounded like that was all he could manage to squeak out.

"Bones?" Wake asked. "Is that what you found?"

"And how were the other villages?" Sylia asked. "Busy at all?"

"Nothing out of the ordinary," Gwyn said as she stepped into the doorway.

"You didn't happen to come across any other visitors while you were out, did you?" Wake asked her.

"Visitors?"

"Leora and Zessa," Desi said.

"We travelled to the island with some friends of ours. They were in these old rickety carts being pulled by those big aquavine," Wake lied. "You couldn't have missed them."

"Oh! Those were visitors? I had no idea. I walked right up and pet their aquavine and everything." Gwyn said with what had suddenly become a sickening smile. "I didn't see the people who owned them, though, so I must have just missed your friends."

Wake knew they were in serious trouble.

"Desi, do it."

"Do what?" the women asked. "Desi?"

Desi cranked the bottom of the small device. A great ball of fire shot out of it, creating a hole in the ceiling of the hut, and launching up into the sky. It let out the loudest squeal Wake had ever heard. The fireworks that fired off near him at the castle weren't even close to the sound the device let out.

He could have chuckled when the fireball burst into a fiery version of the word *HELP*, but the there'd be time for that later. The boy's current situation wasn't a laughing matter.

Wake turned back to the women who each had an angry look on their faces. "We're leaving. Now."

Gwyn's confused anger twisted into a terrifying teeth-bared grin. "Why do you want to leave so soon? Aren't you happy here in paradise?"

"This isn't paradise. This is some freaky pretend village. I don't know who you are or what you want, but you're going to let us leave right now."

"Or what?" Sylia growled. Her kind voice had become deeper than before.

"Or things are going to get really bad for you when our friends actually show up."

"How cute," Gwyn spat. "That was a little cry for help. "We'll just have to be done with you before they arrive."

Wake grabbed Desi and backed up. "Get back out that window when I say so."

The two women started to shake even worse than Desi had when the boy's first arrived on the strange travelling islands. They dropped to the ground and it looked like their bones were changing. Each of them cried out in agony until a pair of wings sprouted out of their backs.

They each stood back up covered in feathers and talons. The kind old woman and her granddaughter were gone. Calling them ordinary people would have been the biggest lie the boys could have told. Now, they had become two bird-women with sinister eyes.

"NOW, DESI!" Wake shouted as he tossed a nearby chair at the women.

They swiped their hands through it, sending splintered wood everywhere. Desi jumped out the window and Wake followed close behind as the two women charged at him.

They laid in a heap and scuttled away from the hut, watching for where the creatures might come from. The village was covered in an eerie quiet. That quiet lasted until the women burst through the roof of the hut and set their sights on the boys.

They shook bits of wood from their raven-haired wings and screeched down at Wake and Desi.

Wake wasn't sure how long it would take for Lady Kohdad and her people to arrive, but he hoped it would be quick. If they didn't make it soon, the boys were going to be the lunch of two hungry harpies.

Chapter 19:
A Wolf in Leora's Clothing

The boys scrambled to their feet and took off toward what would eventually become the crossing between Mulos and Mahlurma. The boiling sun made the run far worse than it otherwise would have been, but there wasn't any time for comfort. The boys needed to stay focused on getting away, and staying alive.

"What are we going to do?" Desi asked.

"No questions. Keep running." Wake made the stupid mistake of glancing backward. "We're headed toward where—Lady Kohdad went. Keep your eyes—open."

"Why—do we—always—end up running?" Desi moaned.

Wake's irritation at his brother gave him a second wind. "If you want to fight the two vicious bird-ladies you're on your own."

They rushed through a set of trees, but that didn't slow the harpies one bit. "You know that making us chase you is only making us hungrier?" One of the harpies said as they flew closer.

"They're going to catch us," Desi said.

"No—they—aren't."

One of the harpies swiped at the boy's ankles, sending them both to the ground.

"Maybe they are." Wake made a quick recovery. "Desi, you alright?"

"Yeah." Desi clutched his ankle. "I think so."

"You won't be for long," the harpies said in unison as they approached.

Wake looked around for anything that could help them, but there weren't even any rocks or sticks on the ground.

Wake stood up and handed his bag to Desi. "The artifact is in there. You need to go get the last one from Voxal."

"It is?" Desi stared at his brother. "Wait—what are you saying?"

"How sweet," one of the harpies cackled. "A noble sacrifice."

"A stupid sacrifice," the other harpy said.

"Listen to me." Wake let out a weak smile. "I'm gonna buy you some time."

"You can't! I won't leave you."

"Please, Desi."

"No. I'm not leaving you."

Wake turned around and shoved him hard. "GET OUT OF HERE!"

The harpies closed in with their teeth bared. "That's enough of this. Neither of you are going anywhere."

Wake stared at Desi, doing everything he could to look angry—to look like he hated him. Whatever it would take to get him to leave Wake behind. All Desi could do was scuttle backward.

"You know," Wake turned to face the harpies. "You two really suck."

"The marrow from your bones?" the harpies spat back. "In due time, child."

"I walked right into that one."

One of the harpies' ears twitched and they turned their attention to a set of nearby bushes. "What is this? An ambush? You creatures—come out now!"

"An ambush?"

One of the harpies rose into the air and swung one of her huge wings in the direction of the bushes. Feathers flew from the wing and shot straight through the bushes. The feathers were somehow sharp enough to slice the bushes apart.

"Some ambush," the other harpy scoffed.

"What just happened?" Desi asked.

"I don't know," Wake snapped.

A low growl started near where the harpy had launched her feathers, and soon the growl sounded as if it was coming from every direction.

"You missed them," the standing harpy said.

"They're all around us," the other said as she landed on the ground.

"What is?" Wake asked.

Huge wolves hopped out of the surrounding bushes and from behind nearby trees. They rushed the harpies and dragged them screaming into the bushes. After a moment of snarling and shouting, everything became quiet.

Wake snatched his bag back from Desi and they both looked around. "What the heck?"

"Were those wolves?" Desi asked.

"They were." Wake grabbed Desi's arm and took a slow step away from where the wolves dragged the harpies. "Stay quiet, and move slowly."

After a few quiet steps, a lone wolf hopped out of the bushes and stared at the boys.

Wake could feel Desi shaking. "Should we run?"

"If we run—" Wake didn't take his eyes off the wolf. "That thing is definitely going to eat us."

The wolf lumbered toward them until Wake could feel the warmth of its breath on his face. Harpies were bad enough, but at least they could outrun them. They had no chance against a wolf that was easily three times bigger than any normal wolf back home.

"What—do—we—do?" Desi whispered.

Wake was at a loss for words as he stared at the wolf's sharp teeth. It sniffed Wake before crumbling to the ground. In a flash of light, the wolf morphed into Leora.

"Lady—Leora?" Wake finally managed to ask.

"How many times are you going to do that? Huh? It's Le—or—a. There's no need to be so formal. Are you two alright?" She ran a hand along Wake's face. "We came as quick as we could."

Wake watched another wolf transform, and Zessa appeared in its spot. "You're—you're all wolf-people? Werewolves?"

"Yup." She ran a finger along her nose. "Easy to keep track of your friends when you have such a sensitive sense of smell. Makes a party full of pigs the worst." She looked back to the bushes they pulled the harpies into. "We usually have a nose for the stench of harpies. They must have had some kind of charm to mask their scent."

"They looked like two ordinary people," Desi said.

"Yeah, we thought they were human—until they tried to eat us," Wake said. "Thanks for coming to help."

The island started to shake, but the dull haze of black smog was enough to signal to Wake that Mulos had connected with Voxal.

Leora smiled. "Looks like you boys need to hurry if you want that Voxal artifact." She waved Zessa over. "How about a ride?"

"A ride?" Desi asked.

"Yes, Lady Kohdad?" Zessa asked as he arrived.

"Take everyone and tell the village elder I'll be a little late. I'm going to take Wake and Desi over to the Voxal crossing. They'll need every spare moment they can get."

Zessa glared at Wake. "Yes, Lady Kohdad."

"Thank you."

Zessa turned into a wolf and rushed off with a dozen other wolves that had all remained hidden. Leora dropped to the floor and turned back into a huge grey wolf. She turned her head as if to tell them to hop on.

"You ready for Voxal, Desi?"

"What about the artifact?"

"Were you not listening back there?"

Desi shook his head. "Everything felt like a blur."

"Well, you didn't see it when you went through my bag?" Wake helped Desi onto Leora's back. "Those two jerks had it the whole time."

"I was a little distracted. A village full of bones and nasty harpies will do that."

"Alright, alright." Wake hopped onto her back and grabbed onto the scruff of her neck. Desi wrapped his arms around Wake. "Okay, Leora. Let's do this."

She nodded and shot forward toward Voxal. With each bound, the black smog grew thicker and thicker. It became harder to breathe the further they went. It quickly became clear why all the nature had left the island of Voxal.

If a human could barely breathe—barely even see in the smog, how could any plants find a way to gather enough sunlight?

Wake set his sights on a distant tower. Lights pierced through the thick haze. He knew that had to be where Conah was. Right at the tippy top.

"We're coming for you Conah."

Chapter 20:
The City of Smog

Thanks to the speed of Leora's wolf form, the boys made it to the gap between the islands in no time. They hopped off and coughed to try to clear their lungs of the thick smog. Wake wondered how long it would take to get used to the smoke. Leora morphed back into her human form and started to cough as well.

Something about the way she coughed seemed worse. Wake remembered her last serious coughing fit, but this time Wake saw a brief flash of red in her hand when she pulled her hand away.

"You okay?" Wake asked.

"Fine," she whispered before she cleared her throat. "Fine." She removed a long scarf she had on and tore it into two halves. "Wrap these around your mouths. It'll help with the smog and hopefully, it'll keep most of the things in Voxal from noticing you're human."

"Sweet." They each took the long pieces of fabric and wrapped them around their mouths. "Any ideas for us?"

"Move quickly. You don't have much time." She looked off toward Mulos. "I must go, but I know you two will do it. You have to."

"Thank you—for everything," Wake said.

She inched closer and gave him a quick kiss. It shocked him, but he didn't mind. If Wake made a list of all the girls he wanted to kiss, Leora would be right at the top, even if she could turn into a wolf.

"I pray we see each other again someday." She morphed back into a wolf and rushed back toward Mulos.

Wake never imagined his first kiss would be with a wolf-girl, but he also never imagined he'd do anything he'd done over the last few days.

"Wow."

"What do you—"

"We have to hurry." Wake pulled Desi hard by the arm toward the city. "We have less than two hours to figure out how to get the artifact on an island where we can barely even see anything."

Desi gave him a sad look before he pulled his scarf over his face, but there wasn't any time to apologize. They needed to keep moving. If they missed their shot, they'd be stuck amongst the islands for another six months.

Voxal was a mess when compared to the other islands. Instead of vibrant nature, the ground was nothing but hard dirt and sand. Rather than being able to hear the churning sounds of the ocean, all that could be heard was the metallic clanking of machinery.

Nothing the boys had heard back home did the sounds of Voxal justice.

They'd only been on the island for a few minutes, but it was already their least favourite one. That was saying something considering they'd been used as lab rats on Cerulea, been actual prisoners on Flurris, and then chased by harpies on Mulos.

"How much worse can this get?" Wake said under his breath.

"What was that?" Desi asked between coughs.

"Nothing—just something I—never mind."

"Can you see anything?"

Wake scanned everything around him, but all he could make out was a dull glow coming from up ahead. "There's something up ahead. A street? Maybe a market?"

The dull light grew bigger and brighter.

HONK!
HONK!
HONK!

Wake looked down—at some point, the dry earth had become a paved road without them noticing. He grabbed Desi and hopped out of the way of the light as a car zoomed past.

"Whoa," Desi said. "They really do have cars here."

"We gotta be careful." Wake helped him up. "We were in such a hurry that we didn't even notice we'd stepped right into the middle of a road." The sounds of people chatting and cars zipping along had mixed in with the machinery. "You hear that? We gotta be close to something."

"What kind of things do you think we'll find here?" Desi asked. "What kinda thing could have driven a car like that?"

"I really don't want to find out." He pointed up at the nearby glow of a tower. "That glow is the tallest one, so it must be Conah's place. Let's just head right there and maybe we can avoid nearly getting eaten again."

They continued toward the tower and the hectic sounds of people and cars grew louder. Eventually, they found themselves in the middle of yet another crowded street fair. There were creatures they recognized from each of the islands, but even more that they had never seen before.

Wake met eyes with a disfigured creature that was covered in oozing lumps. He squeezed Desi's wrist. "Stay close to me."

The streets were filled with grotesque and sickly creatures. There were pigs that were even larger than the ones of Flurris, with folds of fat hanging to the floor. Aquatic creatures from Cerulea whose eyes glowed a dull yellow were darted around the street. There were even spider creatures similar to Ebbie crawling through the streets, but they lacked any of her warm features.

Every single creature looked sick.

Every single creature looked angry.

Every single creature looked dangerous.

"Wake?" Desi whispered.

He could feel Desi starting to slow down as he looked at the surrounding stalls. "Don't stop to look at anything."

They moved to the side with the rest of the crowd as a car made its way through the street. There was no telling if it was someone important, or someone who got lost in the smog.

They made it through the thickest part of the crowd and noticed that the source of much of the light wasn't coming from the surrounding buildings. The lights that shone through the smog were actually coming from street lamps. Whatever the advancements that Voxal had made were, they shared in a lot of the comforts the boys had back home.

"I don't like it here," Desi said.

"Can't blame you there. Me either."

"It reminds me of home, but uglier. Like—when mom takes us into the city."

"Smells about the same." Wake looked around. "I wish we had some way to keep track of the time." He looked up to the sun, but he didn't even need to block out its rays due to the smog. "I can barely even tell where the sun is."

Wake bumped into something while his eyes were on the sky, and both he and Desi tumbled to the floor.

It was a man.

A man with a young red-headed girl.

A well-dressed man with a solid gold wristwatch.

Wake stared into his dark blue eyes through the thick smog. He wasn't quite sure why, but he knew exactly who he was looking up at.

"Conah."

The man looked down his nose at Wake. He adjusted his hat and smirked. "Didn't I tell you I had my own fan club, Mari?"

The young girl stared at Desi without saying a word.

Wake and Desi stood up, and they each pulled down their scarves. "So you are Conah?"

"In the flesh. Who are—" Something changed. It was like he looked at the boys for the first time. "Other humans."

"That's right."

"How refreshing. Oz," Conah snapped his fingers. "Eighty-six these boys—all the way."

A burly hand landed on each of the boys.

Wake had no idea what eighty-six meant, but it couldn't have been good.

Chapter 21:
Callous Conah

"Wait! You can't do this! We came all this way," Wake said as he struggled against the brute strength of the half-bull half-man named Oz.

Conah looked as if he was considering Wake's words for a moment. He held up a hand. "Hold up, Oz." He stepped closer. "I've decided I'd like to hear what they have to say."

"Sure thing, boss." Oz let go of the boys and gave them a shove toward Conah. "Touch the boss, and you won't like what happens to you."

"What we have to say?" Desi asked.

"You said you came all this way. You must have something to say to me, no?"

Wake gulped. "We—we need your artifact."

"My artifact?"

"Don't play stupid. We know you have it."

"You know I have an artifact?" He looked from the boys to Oz and then over to the girl he was with. "An artifact? What is this artifact supposed to be?"

Conah looked like he had no idea what Wake was talking about. It had to be an act. There was no way he wasn't aware of the Voxal artifact. He's human, which means he must have been searching for a way home at some point.

Right?

"Well—we—uh—we don't really know what it looks like," Wake stammered.

"You came all the way here. Two boys. All alone." He gave the boys an amused look. "And you don't even know what the artifact I'm supposed to have is?"

"Yes?" Desi said.

"And if I don't even know what you're talking about —which I absolutely do not—what are you planning on doing then?"

Wake could feel himself becoming angry. "We don't have time for games. We need to get back to Mahlurma before the islands separate."

Desi tugged at Wake's sleeve. "Wake, what if Dub was wrong?"

"What do you mean?"

"Maybe wrong isn't the right word. If Conah really is being honest, and he really doesn't know what the artifact is, that could be why no one has any idea what it is."

"Sure, but Amphinara—"

"Told us just as much as Dub did."

Wake didn't want to admit it, but Desi was right. Dub had just mentioned that Conah keeps the artifact close, but no one had seen it. Amphinara said it was with Conah in his tower. Neither of them was able to tell them what it looked like.

Conah moved closer and crouched down. "Guys, I can tell this is really rough." He gestured around. "This whole island adventure must be one of the most difficult things you've ever done. I get it. Hell, I was you guys— had a few more people with me, but I was you guys."

"So?"

"So—I'll have Oz here, eighty-six you guys. Just get rid of the whole headache I'm sure everything's been."

Oz's heavy hands slapped back down onto them. Wake scowled at Conah as he walked away. "What's eighty-six mean?"

"Oh, I'm so sorry." He stopped and faced them again with a twisted grin. "Oz is going to toss you into the ocean."

"You can't!" Desi cried.

"The islands are all connected." Wake smirked. "What? Is he gonna babysit us until they split apart again?"

Conah rubbed his hands together. "These kids are fiery. I like it!" He sighed. "No, kid. You see right where Mahlurma, Mulos, and Voxal all meet together, there's this little—teeny-tiny hole."

"A hole?"

"A hole. A pit. God's toilet. Whatever you want to call it. A big ole opening between the islands." He pat Wake on the head. "And now Oz is gonna chuck you in it, so I don't need to deal with you two anymore."

"Daddy, you can't!" the red-headed girl cried.

"Sweetheart," Conah said as he put a hand on her head. "What's the matter?"

"They're human like us! You can't throw them away!"

Conah positioned himself so that he could see the boys, and the girl was faced away from them. "I know they're human, sweetheart, but humans are greedy. They want what we have here, and we can't have that. We are on a mission, and what does daddy say about the mission?"

"Nothing can get in the way until it's done."

"Very good, sweetheart." Conah gave Oz a serious look and cocked his head. "Now how's about we go get you some of that tasty ice cream, huh?"

Oz tossed each of the boys over his shoulder and made his way through the city. It didn't matter how much they fought—he was too strong. It didn't matter how much they shouted and screamed—no one on Voxal cared.

"What are we gonna do?" Desi asked.

"I don't know if there's anything we can do."

"Nope!" Oz replied with a hearty laugh. "You two are done for. Trust me, this isn't the first time I've done something like this."

"You know, you could not throw us into the ocean," Wake snapped.

"But it'll be so much fun."

"Not for us."

Oz raised an eyebrow. "Do you really think I care about how much fun something is for you?"

"Why are you taking orders from that guy anyway?" Desi asked.

"Why?" Oz shrugged. "Does it look like I have anything better to do?"

"I hope you take this as offensively as possible—" Wake thought back to his experience on Singo's farm. "You have the brain of a talking fruit."

"You—you calling me stupid?" Oz asked, sounding a bit hurt.

"Entirely. Literally as dumb as a piece of fruit. You actually said pretty much the same thing that a pear once said to me."

"I'm—I'm not as stupid as a pear." Wake could feel Oz's grip tighten. "Take that back."

"No. You're probably actually *dumber* than a piece of fruit. At least the fruit we met were helpful."

"Yeah, you can't even think for yourself." Desi started laughing. Wake wasn't sure if he had caught on to what he was trying to do, but he was helping regardless. "You could crush Conah, but instead you just follow his orders. You're just a sidekick."

Wake could see the split between the islands that Conah was talking about. If they couldn't find a way to get free soon, they'd be taking a permanent swim.

"You don't know what Conah's done for me."

"Whatever he's done is enough for you to toss two kids into the ocean?" Wake asked. "Have half a brain."

"Well—I—he—you see—" He stopped at the edge of the pit, but to Wake's surprise, he set them down. "You kids are really hurtful, you know that?" He wiped a tear from his eye.

"Are you crying?" Desi asked.

"I'm not."

"You are crying." Wake grinned.

"No, I'm not."

"Yes, you are," the boys said together.

"NO, I'M NOT." Oz started wiping the tears that were falling from his face.

Desi hopped down between his legs and Wake understood immediately. It was one of the last things the two of them had watched on television before they ventured out into the forest. To get back at their school bully, one boy acted as a block and the other pushed the bully, sending him tumbling into a fountain.

Wake slammed his body into Oz as hard as he could, and Oz tumbled over Desi. Luckily, Oz's flailing legs knocked Wake backward, keeping him from joining Oz in the water below.

He crawled away from the pit. "Holy crap." He looked over to Desi. "Did that just happen?"

Desi didn't look excited at their victory over the monstrous Oz. He looked—sad almost. without a word to Wake, he stood up and made his way to the edge of the pit.

Desi stared off into the hole between the islands. "What did we do?"

"Desi? What?" Wake didn't understand.

It was either going to be Oz or it was going to be them.

Desi looked back at Wake with tears in his eyes. "What did we just do?"

Chapter 22:
Brothers Fight

Wake crept to the edge of the pit and stared down at the swirling waters. Oz wasn't anywhere to be seen. A part of him felt bad about what had happened, but another part of him didn't care at all.

He was ready to toss them in, why shouldn't they have been ready to do the same?

"Desi?" Wake put a hand on his shoulder. "You okay?"

"Don't touch me." He shook it off. "We shouldn't have done that—I can't believe I did that. Why did I do that?"

"Don't tell me you feel sorry for that thing." Wake tried to get a hint of what was going on in Desi's head. "That was a great idea. We didn't have any other plays."

"He didn't throw us in." Desi pushed Wake hard. "He put us down." He pushed him again. "He was talking to us."

"Stop it. He would have ended up throwing us in anyway. You heard him—he said he'd done it before." Wake pushed Desi's arms away as he moved in to push him again. "Do you want to get home or not?"

"Not if it means we're as bad as the rest of these monsters." Desi gave Wake a hard shove, sending him backward again.

He was surprised by Desi's strength. It had been a while since they'd done any play fighting, so Wake wasn't used to the kind of power Desi was displaying. He had a feeling that most of Desi's strength was coming from his anger. Wake's tired legs didn't help the situation.

"Push me again—"

Desi came closer with tears in his eyes, ready to give him another hard shove. Wake deflected his arms again, but this time gave him a wicked shove right back. Desi flew backward and looked back at Wake, his face red with anger.

"I warned you, Desi. Cut it out."

"WE KILLED HIM!" Desi screamed at Wake.

"What do you want from me? Do you even want to get home? Are you even aware of just how much the people around us have sacrificed just to give us a chance to get home?"

"We killed him."

"The ocean did," Wake spat.

"We pushed him into the ocean."

"Just like he was going to do to us." Wake started to pace. "Did you forget what Ebbie and Dub did for us? What Twig did for us? What Lady Kohdad did for us?" He studied Desi as he stood up, his face still covered with anger. "What about Aza? Did you forget that Aza might actually be dead right now? Why? Because he gave everything he had to make sure we made it home. If we just gave up and let some bull-man toss us to our doom when we had a way out, we'd be spitting on Aza's legacy."

"I shouldn't have done what I did," Desi grumbled.

"Well, you did it, and you can't take it back. You can regret it all you want, Desi, but the truth—the hard truth—is that when we get home, everything we've done here—it isn't going to matter. Not one bit. For all you know, that freak just got transported to another world.

Remember? JUST LIKE WE DID WHEN WE FELL INTO WATER."

"You're wrong."

Wake almost didn't hear what Desi had said. It was a quick whisper—an angry whisper.

"What?"

"You're wrong." Desi took his bag off and threw it at Wake. "Everything we did here is going to matter. It's going to matter to me. I have to live with what we just did, and so do you."

"I was starting to think you were growing up here. That you were starting to smarten up, but you're nothing but a stupid kid still, Desi."

"Mom would be so disappointed in you," Desi said.

"You know what? She might be, but if we did nothing, she wouldn't have anyone to be disappointed in." Wake kicked Desi's bag back at him. "Why don't you just go back to Mahlurma. I'll go find the last artifact on my own."

The islands shook with a force neither of the boys had felt before, sending them both to the ground. Before they made it back to their feet, the islands had begun to pull away from one another. Their time on Voxal was up.

"Wake?"

"Desi?"

The islands pulled further and further apart.

The islands pulled the *boys* further and further apart.

"WAKE!"

"DESI!"

There wasn't any way to get to each other.

"NO!" Wake looked for something—anything—any way to reach Desi. "NO, NO, NO!"

Mahlurma pulled even further from Voxal, and Desi disappeared in the thick black smog.

"DESI!"

"WAKE!"

"DESI!"

"WAKE!"

"DESI!"

"WAKE!"

"DESI!"

"DESI!"

There was nothing.

No response.

Just the sound of the ocean waves below.

"DESI!"

"DESI, PLEASE!"

Still nothing.

A simple breeze broke Wake's heart.

Wake dropped to his knees.

Alone, he stared off toward the smoggy island.

Desi was gone.

Gone...

Chapter 23:
Six Long Months

It had been nearly six months since Wake and Desi were separated. Actually, it would be exactly six months in just one day. Wake had counted the days since they were separated. He would finally get his chance to save his little brother.

Something gnawed at him.

Wake had no idea if Desi was okay. He was trapped all by himself on Voxal. It was rare for Desi to go anywhere without Wake, so all Wake could think about was situation after situation that left Desi helpless.

Those awful creatures.

That thick, sickening smog.

All the creepy industrial buildings.

The never-ending screeching of old machinery.

Desi had to survive it all on his own.

No one to love.

No one to trust.

"Wake? You alright, sweetie?" Ebbie asked as she rested a hand on his shoulder.

"Sorry. I must have zoned out again."

"You've been doing that more and more lately." She gave him a concerned look. "Dub and I have been talking about everything surrounding you boys."

Wake tossed his half-eaten meal out the window to the aquavine, and put his bowl on the counter. "What about it?"

"We're going to come with you to Voxal. We were even thinking of asking the other villagers—"

He spun around. "Seriously? Now you want to help?"

Maybe a tiny part of Wake meant to lash out at Ebbie, but he didn't want to make her feel bad. It wasn't her or Dub's fault that he and Desi had to go on a big adventure. It wasn't their fault that he and Desi fought.

It wasn't their fault that—

"Wake," Ebbie gave him a hurt look. "We want to help put things right—all of us do. You won't have a lot of time to find him, so three, no—a whole village of heads will be better than one."

"And what? What if we can't find him?" Wake felt his face getting hot with anger. "What am I supposed to do? Go home and abandon my little brother? Leave him stuck in a land full of monsters forever?"

Wake's emotions took over and despite an attempt to stifle yet another set of tears, they fought their way out. The uncontrollable sobs took over, which was something Wake hadn't become used to despite the fact that they were, at minimum, a weekly occurrence.

Ebbie rushed over and threw her arms around him, but he pushed her off. "What if he's gone?"

Ebbie rubbed the side of his face. "He's not gone, Wake."

"How can you be sure?"

"I just—" She looked out the window toward Voxal. "I just am. He's young, and maybe a bit meek, but he's a smart boy. He's your little brother, but you've done an excellent job helping him grow into himself."

"Grow into himself?"

She nodded. "Everyone has to do it sometime or another. You did it so fast, faster than a young boy should have to. Some do it because of tragedy—some out of necessity due to their situation. That's you. Because of that, you've been able to help Desi along."

Dub burst through the door. "Wake. I need to borrow you for a second."

He sighed. "Okay, but if it's another aquavine having a baby, I'll sit this one out."

"No." Dub looked serious, but it was masked with a big smile. "I have someone here who would like to speak with you."

Desi.

It had to be.

Who else would know where Wake was?

Leora? Twig?

He rushed past Dub and Ebbie, and out to the village. The village was quiet, and there was no sign of Desi. There wasn't any sign of anyone.

"What? I thought you said—"

Dub snorted. "Excited little lad." He pointed up. "Up there."

Wake looked up to see the silhouette of a strange bird flying in the sky. It spotted them and made its way to the ground. As it landed, it became clear that it wasn't just a simple bird. It was actually a strange long-bodied raccoon with a large pair of wings. The creature's face made him think of Aza, but his posture reminded him of a high school kid.

Dub had gone on a journey to find Aza, but when he came back he wasn't all that interested in sharing what he had found out. Wake had a feeling he knew what that meant.

"Hey, you must be—Wake?" the raccoon asked in a dull voice.

"Who's asking?"

176

It pulled a piece of paper from its bag and handed it to him. "Delivery for Wake."

Without another word, it took off into the sky in the direction of Voxal.

"Thanks?" Wake looked from the strange creature to the note in his hands. It had his name written on it in fancy writing.

"Well?" Dub asked. "What are you waiting for? Open it."

"I don't get it." He wiggled the note. "Who'd be sending me mail? You don't think Desi would—"

Dub put a hand on his hand. "Open it."

Wake pulled a small seal open and unfolded the paper—

Wake,

I believe I am in possession of something you are interested in. If you'd like to claim said possession, you will meet me tomorrow at the crossing between Mahlurma and Voxal. I have a feeling you'd like to get home, so I suggest you aren't late.

~ Conah

"What does it say?" Dub asked as Ebbie came out to join them. "Who's it from?"

"It's from Conah."

"Conah?" Ebbie gasped. "Why would Conah be sending you a letter?"

"He says he has something I want. Something to help me get home."

"The last artifact."

Wake nodded.

"But no mention of Desi?"

"No." Wake crumpled the letter. "Conah wants to meet me at the crossing tomorrow."

"Does he now?" Dub crossed his arms. "Well, I'll be sure to gather anyone from the village who wants to help. We Mahlurmites aren't going to let him intimidate and bully you."

"Really?"

"Of course. You're one of us, and we here protect our own," Dub nudged him. "Even if they're human."

He looked up at them and smiled. "Thanks guys."

Wake looked off toward Voxal. Something about it seemed different. It was the smog. It wasn't quite as thick as it had been all the other times he'd looked toward the island. Over the last six months, the production of smog has seemed to almost slow down.

Wake was actually able to distinguish between the smog and the buildings, even from the distance. He figured it wasn't worth asking about. Every business had its slow times of the year, and maybe that time was now for Voxal.

It didn't matter how dirty or clean Voxal was.

It didn't matter what Conah had up his sleeve.

All that mattered was finding Desi, getting the last artifact, and heading home once and for all.

One way or another, the next day was going to be Wake's last day in that strange world.

Chapter 24:
How I Missed You

Wake had never shaken the way he had as he waited for Mahlurma and Voxal to connect. He wasn't sure why he was anxious, but he knew why he was scared. There was no telling what someone like Conah was up to. He and Desi had done so much to claim the other artifacts, so there was no way Conah planned on just handing it over to him.

Off in the distance, Conah was already waiting by an elongated car—like a limo, but without the sleek design. Being the head of Voxal, he must have brought along some kind of security force with a huge car like that.

Ebbie Squeezed his hand. "It's going to be okay."

Wake looked back at the crowd of villagers who had shown up to support him. "I know it is."

He'd gotten to know some of them during his six-month stay on Mahlurma, but he hadn't spoken once to most of them. Having that kind of support gave him newfound confidence.

"Don't forget to thank them for me." Wake smiled at Ebbie.

"Of course."

The islands began to shake as they made contact. Wake didn't move a muscle this time. He'd made a point to head to each connection point every time Mahlurma connected to Cerulea and Mulos in order to practice his stability. The shaking may have been fierce, but he wasn't going to move an inch.

He knew there wasn't any room for mistakes.

His eyes burned a hole into Conah as the shaking stopped. He held a hand up to the villagers before he stepped to the edge of the connection alone. He could see an amused look written across Conah's face.

"You've got something for me?" Wake asked.

Conah didn't look exactly how he remembered, though. His short hair was now long and tied back into a frizzy ponytail. Even his skin seemed different—like he hadn't gone outside since the last time they'd come face to face.

Conah stopped short, and the two stared at one another, each on their own island. "Wake, it's good to see you."

"I'd say I feel the same, but I'm not big on lying."

"The same as ever." Conah laughed. "I guess more has changed than I thought."

Wake raised an eyebrow. "What are you going on about?"

"You don't recognize me? Not even a little?"

"Recognize you?" Wake cocked his head in confusion.

He studied Conah, but he looked the same as he remembered. The same shiny shoes, the same pinstriped suit, the same—well, not the same hair. His hair was frizzier, almost like Desi's.

He looked closer.

The eyes weren't the same either.

Conah's eyes were blue.

Now his eyes were hazel.

Just like—

"Desi?" Wake inched closer. "Desi, is that you?"

He smiled. "Took you long enough, *big* brother. Although, I guess I'm the big brother now, huh?"

He took a knee so Wake could see him better. There wasn't any question. Conah was Desi.

But how?

Wake wrapped him in a massive hug. "Desi, I—I'm so sorry. I—"

Desi hugged him tighter than anyone ever had. "Stop. It's okay. Brother's fight. Especially big stupid ones like us."

"It's only been six months." He pulled back. "How —how did you—how are you so *old?* You're like the same age as mom."

"Hey! Watch it." Desi chuckled. "I figured out pretty quick that time moves differently on Voxal when after a second birthday, the islands still hadn't connected again."

"How is that possible?" Wake asked, but all Desi replied with was a shrug. "How long? How long were you on your own?"

"Apparently the length of time is different each time the islands separate, but I'd say, give or take—" He sighed. "Thirty years."

"Thirty years?!"

It sounded impossible, but the longer Wake looked at him, the more certain he was that it was really Desi.

"What did you do?" Wake asked. "How are you Conah all the sudden?"

"After our fight, I wasn't really sure what to do. I had no idea how I was supposed to survive on my own." He looked up to the sky. "I thought maybe I'd steal the last artifact from Conah and figure out a way to fly over to Mahlurma, but all those winged raccoons are so lazy."

"Trust me. I could tell."

"When I went to snag the artifact, Conah and his goons caught me. I figured I was done for, but he actually got really upset when I explained what had happened—

181

that and he was impressed that we took out Oz." He ran his hand across a gold watch he was wearing. "Apparently he had gone through something similar when he was a boy, but the person he was with had abandoned him completely. We never heard from them again."

Wake rubbed his arm. "You were his apprentice then? Helping him with all those smoggy machines?"

"Helping him *fix* those smoggy machines."

"Fix them?"

"I guess it's not going quite as well or as quickly as I'd hoped." He glanced back toward Voxal. "Conah and I started working on cleaning up the nasty smog the machines and factories were producing. Sometime in the next fifteen years, all that smog should be gone."

The smog had been clearing puff by puff. Whatever it was they had been doing, it really was working.

"And then what?"

"I'm not sure." Desi kicked some dirt. "A continued focus on cleaner production to welcome nature back to Voxal. Then pointing our eyes toward the future of the other islands."

"The other islands? They don't have any machines or factories."

"Not yet." Desi's expression melted into one of sadness. "But they will. We need to be ready to help them when that happens so they don't make the same mistakes as the people of Voxal. We need to protect these beautiful islands—all these wonderful people—from stumbling down the same bleak path."

"You think you can do that?"

"I do." Desi picked up a handful of dirt. "We get out of the planet what we put in. If all we do is continue to harm it, one day it will fight back." He dumped the dirt back to the ground. "A fight we can't win."

Wake smiled. "I'm really proud of you, Desi."

Desi smiled back before his attention slipped behind Wake. "I know we don't have a lot of time, and we have a lot to talk about, but do you think I could say hello to Ebbie and Dub?"

"Of course." Wake waved them over. "They'll be so excited to find out it's you. They were going to help me find you—all of the villagers were."

Desi looked a bit choked up. "Really?"

"Is everything alright, Wake?" Ebbie asked.

"Ebbie, Dub, I want to reintroduce you to Desi." Wake gestured toward him.

Both of their eyes went wide. "Desi?!"

He smiled. "In the flesh."

"You're so big now! I'm going to need to make double the pie!" Ebbie said as she wrapped him in a hug.

Dub patted Wake's shoulder. "I knew we'd find him." He headed over and hugged Desi. "Looks like you've grown into a fine man. I should have suspected that you were the one changing that place for the better when I finally managed to see the buildings through the smog for the first time in years."

"So you can see a difference!" Desi laughed. "I'm glad." He looked back to his car. "I have a surprise for everyone."

He let out a loud whistle and the car door flung open. Out stepped Aza and Twig. Neither of them looked like they'd aged a day, but their eyes lit up when they spotted everyone.

"No way," Wake said, fighting the urge to run to them. "They've been with you all this time?"

"Well, negotiating the release of Aza from that hog was a pain thanks to the messengers, but I managed it eventually with enough coaxing." He nudged Twig as he and Aza made it over. "Plus, who better to run my personal security than the slyest person I know."

Wake shook Twig's hand. "Thanks for taking care of my brother."

He nodded and stepped back. "Anytime." He pulled a small instrument from his bag and tossed it to him. "That's for you."

"I thought you said this was the last thing you had of your family?"

He pulled his own version of the instrument out. "I made you your own, just like I said I would."

Desi grinned. "I've gotten pretty good at it."

"Well, you've had enough practice, old man," Twig said with a laugh.

"Watch it."

Aza jumped on Wake. "Thanks for abandoning me, kid."

"You were the one who made Twig toss you!" Wake would have been worried about a comment like that if Aza hadn't hugged him so tight. "We just wanted to give you a chance to save yourself. Dub went to find you, but you weren't in Flurris anymore. Where did you go?"

"I'm sure." He shot Wake a sideways look as he climbed to the ground. "What can I say? The Hog King was so impressed by what I'd done that he wanted to keep me around as a prisoner-storyteller. Eventually, a pack of mailmen flew in and carried me to Voxal and that's where I met up with Desi. If I'm being totally honest, I figured I was done for."

"And you didn't have them fly you back here?"

"They barely made it over to Voxal."

"Trust me when I say," Desi cut in. "You do not want to try to deal with those lazy things. Pretty much the only peaceful sentient things with wings and they practically refuse to fly anywhere."

Aza nodded. "A couple years isn't a big deal anyway."

"A couple years? How old are you?" Wake asked.

Aza brought a finger to his chin. "Just over five hundred, I think."

"Whoa."

He looked over toward Ebbie. "Ms. Ebbie! Dub!" He hopped into the arms of Ebbie and Dub and the three of them had a tear-filled reunion.

Desi rubbed his neck. "I tried to bring Shof too, but he's surprisingly hard to find. I guess he really does keep on moving."

"What about Leora—Lady Kohdad?"

"Oh." Desi hung his head. "Remember that cough she had?" Wake nodded. "It was more serious than most people thought."

"Is she—?"

"No. I received word that she's weak, and bedridden, but she did send me a message to give you her regards. She really was upset she wouldn't be able to come today."

Wake sighed. "At least she's okay."

"You made quite the impression on her."

Wake's face became hot. "Shut up."

Desi pulled something small out of his pocket. It looked like a piece of paper, but something felt different about it. The glossy sheen told Wake exactly what it was. It was a picture.

"I wanted to show you this." He held the picture out.

It was a picture of Desi with a woman he didn't know. "Who is this?"

He smiled. "That's my wife—your sister-in-law. Although, I guess that name doesn't really work here. I suppose it makes sense that you don't recognize her at first either."

"Your wife?" Wake studied the picture. The curly red hair, combined with Desi's comment meant the woman could only be one person—even though he had only seen her the one time. "Conah's daughter."

"Mari." Desi nodded.

"Wow."

He was having a hard time finding any words to say. The lost time was eating away at Wake.

"Thirty years. You were on your own for so long. Now we gotta get back and explain everything to mom. I don't know how we're even going to begin to have this make sense. You can even bring Mari, right?"

"About that," Desi frowned. "I can't come home with you."

"What? What are you saying? The last six months, all I could think about was how I was going to find you—how I was going to get you back."

"I know, I know." He sighed and pulled out a small vial of glowing water. "I've started too much to leave now, especially with Mari. I need to stay here and see to it that Voxal cleans its act up. We'll get all the nature to come back, and then like I said, we'll protect the other islands, but we can't figure it out if I'm not here." He tossed the vial to Wake. "That's the—"

"The final artifact." He stared at the vial. "I can't leave without you. What am I supposed to tell mom?"

"You can, and you will." Desi put a hand on his shoulder. "I had a magical little meeting with Amphinara. She's assured me that once you return, it'll be like I never existed. All memory of me will be gone completely."

"All memory? Even my memories?"

He looked away. "I don't know."

"No." Wake clutched the vial. "I can't forget you. I won't forget you."

Desi messed up Wake's hair. "You better not. These islands aren't the only thing that need help." He looked off toward the distant ocean. "Our world—our home—it needs help too. I'll be leaving that job to you."

Wake nodded. "I'll do my best."

"I know you will."

"But first, you gotta tell me all about your life. I want to hear everything."

He sat on the ground. "Take a seat. This'll take a while."

Even though they had two hours together, it felt as if fifteen minutes' worth of storytelling had passed when Desi stood up. Wake was looking at him in an entirely new way. His younger brother had been through a lifetime of struggles on his own and he came out stronger for it.

It inspired Wake.

It would be hard, but if Desi could do it, he knew he could too.

Desi looked at his watch. "It's about time to say goodbye."

"This is it? I'll never see you again?" Tears filled Wake's eyes again. "No goodbye for now?"

"No goodbyes for now. So long—because we'll always be connected. We'll always be brothers." He hugged Wake. "You better not get home and forget that —you got it, Wake?"

Wake hugged him back. "I promise you, I'll never forget you."

Desi's watch started to beep and he took a step back from the crack. "Hug mom for me."

Wake stepped back as well. "I will."

The islands started to shake and they pulled away from one another.

Desi and Twig waved. "See ya, Aza! See ya, Ebbie! See ya, Dub!"

Wake looked back as they all gave a tearful wave. It almost seemed strange to see them cry. He guessed that time didn't matter when it came to these sorts of things, one person can have the same impact in a day that others only have after years.

Wake remained on the edge of the island, watching Desi disappear into the distance until all that he could see was the light smog of Voxal.

He looked down at the vial in his hand and turned toward his Mahlurma family. "Time to go home."

Chapter 25:
The Last Glass Flower

Wake stumbled back to the fields of magnificent glass flowers, still in a daze. It was wonderful to at least have the chance to see his brother when he wasn't even sure if he would be alive, but losing him forever was a hurt that would last a lifetime.

Ebbie, Dub, and Aza had all offered to come along with him to the field to see him off, but Wake felt like this was something he needed to do on his own. It was already a hard day, and having to emotionally fight through leaving his new family to go back to his mom would have only made it harder.

He looked around the field. "I guess this is pretty much where we appeared." He opened his bag and pulled out all the artifacts. "Let's try to not screw this up."

The sudden sound of a familiar cart rolling on the pathways caught Wake's ear. He knew who he hoped it was, but there was no way, right?

He stood up and looked around as Shof came over a hill with his cart of strange ostriches.

"Shof!"

"Huh?!" The happy golden retriever stuck its head out. "Friend!"

Wake almost laughed when he heard the thumping of Shof's tail against the wood of the cart. "What are you doing all the way out here?"

"Shof always on the move."

"Yeah, but why here?"

Shof pulled the cart to a stop next to Wake. "Glass flowers nice. Sharp, but nice." He cocked his head as he looked at Wake's collection of items. "What you doing, friend? Where's littler friend?"

"I—uh—I'm actually about to head home," Wake said, ignoring Shof's second question.

"Where home? Village? I can give friend a ride back. Shof always happy to help."

"No. I know Shof, thanks. I'm headed to my home, which is really far away."

"Really far? Maybe Shof visit one day?"

Wake knew Shof hadn't intended to make him sad, but he could feel himself becoming emotional all over again.

"I'd really like that, but I don't think that'll be happening."

"Why not?"

"It's *really* far."

"Over the ocean far?"

He nodded. "Over the ocean far."

"That far." Shof hopped down off the cart and stretched out his arms. "Friends have to say goodbye. Whether Shof sees you in one week, or one year, or never again. Shof always says goodbye to his friends."

Wake hugged him. "Goodbye, Shof."

"Friend stay safe, okay?"

"I will. You too." Wake let go and Shof hopped back into his cart. "I hope I get to hear all about your adventures one day. I bet you've got lots of stories to tell."

"Shof does live an exciting life." He grabbed the reins, but paused for a moment. "Anyone like me at the very far home?"

"Not in my home," Wake smiled. "But I hope I find a friend like you in my home one day."

He smiled back. "You will. Shof knows it." He snapped the reins and the ostriches took off into the air.

Through all the good and the bad, Wake really was going to miss the islands.

Wake watched his strange, furry friend disappear into the endless blue sky. "This is one weird place."

The strange assortment of items he had poured out of his bag. He never would have guessed that the way to get home would involve a strange plate, a key, an orb, a bag of seeds, and some water.

He set the plate from Mulos on the ground and sprinkled the Mahlurma seeds onto it. "Okay, now the sphere and water." He placed the treasure of Flurris on top of the seeds and dribbled the water from the vial Desi had given him onto everything. "How did anyone ever figure this out?"

He pulled out the key Aphinara had given him "I guess the last step's the weirdest of all." He paused for a moment. "The last step. Then it's back home."

He held the key against the sphere and pretended to turn a lock, but nothing happened.

He held his breath.

More nothing.

"That was it. I followed the steps exactly." He screwed up his hair in frustration. "Maybe I should have just brought Dub and Ebbie with me." He tossed the key at the ground. "Stupid key. Stupid me. Why did I think any of this would work? What would a bunch of monsters know about helping a human get home?"

The key bounced along the ground and landed on the plate with all of the other artifacts. The key started to glow which caught Wake's eye. It disappeared in a burst of light.

"What? What just happened? Did I break it?"

The orb started to glow and soon all of the other artifacts followed suit. The bright light hurt his eyes, but it was so mesmerizing that he couldn't look away.

The light shifted and began to stretch into the sky. Wake tried to figure out what was happening. Maybe some kind of door was forming?

After a moment the light dulled until all that was left was a giant glass flower. "Huh."

He looked around, but all the fields of glass flowers had vanished. All that remained was that one massive flower. When he turned back around all he saw was a white void and a single glass flower. He did a full three-hundred and sixty degree turn to find that all there was now was a white void. He wasn't in that field anymore.

Wake ran his hand along the stem of the glass flower. He suddenly felt sleepy—more tired than he'd ever felt. His eyelids became heavy, and it was as if his body was begging him to lay down.

He curled up underneath the flower and looked up at its sparkling petals one final time.

"Everyone—thank you for looking out for me—for Desi. Ebbie, Dub, Aza, Amphinara, Twig, Shof, none of you had any reason to help us, but you did anyway. I couldn't forget any of you if I tried."

His eyes closed. He tried to open them, but they stayed shut. He could feel the subtle allure of sleep pulling him into a dark void.

In the next moment—

Everything went black.

Chapter 26:
The Way Things Were

When Wake opened his eyes, he found himself lying by the edge of the stream he and Desi had fallen into all those months ago.

What was strange, was that Wake felt as if no time had truly passed. The weather and time of day were exactly what he remembered from the day they had been transported to those strange islands. He was even back in his raincoat from all those months ago.

Not *everything* was how it had been.

Desi was still gone.

He wasn't thrashing about in the water.

The tracks he'd made through the muddy forest floor as he slipped and tumbled into the stream weren't even there anymore.

Wake was alone.

He sat up and looked around. Same old forest, yet somehow, almost completely different. He felt something in his hand, and he smiled when he found it was the instrument Twig had given him.

He looked around and brought the instrument to his lips. He focused on a nearby tree branch and began to play the tune Twig had taught him.

"Huh. No forest spirits." He looked over a couple of dead trees. "It must be hard for them to want to come out in a world like this."

"Wake?" his mother called from the direction of home. "Time to come in. Dinner's ready!"

Wake stood up and took a breath. He wasn't sure what was about to happen. "Uh—mom? Does anything feel—different?"

There was a pause.

"Different? What are you talking about?" she called back. "Hurry up or dinner's going to get cold."

Wake couldn't bring himself to ask about Desi. Not yet. The thought that all memory of him really was gone was terrifying.

"Uh—never mind. I'm—I'm coming!" Wake started toward his mother, but something glinting in the sun caught his eye.

It was a single glass flower growing right on the bank of the stream.

There was no telling if it was really there on the river, some small piece of the islands that had travelled with him, or just his mind playing tricks on him.

He inched toward it, watching the colour of the glass shift as the sunlight passed through it. His mind wasn't playing tricks on him. The glass flower was really there.

He picked it and twirled it in his fingers like he had the first time he and Desi found them. "How'd you get here?"

Part of him wanted to keep the flower in secret. Another part of him wanted to release the flower, letting it float into the sky as a kind of final send-off for the brother the world had forgotten.

A brother he'd never forget.

He twisted the flower's stem in his fingers, and lifted it into the air, letting it float into the sky above. He watched as it spun and danced its way through the trees.

As if the world itself wanted the flower to travel to the heavens, the dark clouds began to part, and the flower headed up to the deep blue.

Wake watched as it disappeared into the endless sky, a smile on his face, and a single tear streaming down his cheek.

"So long, Desi."

He headed back toward home, but a strong wind gust stopped him in his tracks. He turned around, and swore he saw what looked like a young grey wolf on the opposite side of the river—but there was nothing there. He was back home, but he knew his friends were still watching over him.

He turned, wondering if he should even try to tell his mom about what he'd experienced, but another slight breeze caught his attention—

So long, Wake.

The End.

Check out the other novels
written by
Cameron Stewart Miller:
(Available in paperback and EBOOK on
Amazon)

Intercepting Fate - Book One: Extinction Virus

The greatest hero the world has ever known is dead, and a new strain of the Extinction Virus is on the horizon.

After Rhys York, a young boxer from the slums of Sellea City puts his life on the line during a raging house fire, he earns himself an opportunity to become a hero. A team of technologically enhanced heroes known as Interceptors are holding tryouts to find their newest member, but becoming a hero is anything but simple. Along with his best friend Kieran, Rhys battles it out against hundreds of potential recruits in order to become not only the world's newest hero but also the new partner to the most advanced AI in existence, Ayla.

Everyone may dream of one day being a hero that the world can look up to, but Rhys has different goals. Being a hero is great, but getting revenge against the monster that murdered his parents would be even better. Luckily, Rhys's goal lines up with the goal of the Interceptors as the man who killed his parents also happens to be the team's greatest foe, a man known only as Zeal.

Scallywags

Is this ship sinking?

That's what Finn thought right before learning one of the most closely guarded pirate secrets ever whispered across the seas.

When Finn was just a boy, his sleepy village was ravaged by a band of horrific pirates. The destruction they left behind was nothing compared to what they had taken – Finn's mother. After years of wondering what happened to her, Finn finds an opportunity to set out in search of his long-lost mother with some help from the most notorious pirate captain to sail the seas, Captain Fortune Palmer.

Finn's only problem is that Fortune isn't exactly what he'd imagined from all the stories he'd heard.

With his furry companion by his side, Finn sets out into the exciting and dangerous world of swashbuckling adventure. Between Pirate Hunters, scorned ex-lovers, and ancient warriors with magical treasure, Finn has his hands full as he works to discover what became of his mother the day she was taken while also proving his worth to his legendary captain.

Getting Locked Down

On what was supposed to be the happiest day of his life, Brain Berkley gets ditched at the altar by his fiancee, Sarah for one of the douchiest guys around.

Sappy, I know, but a chance meeting with a mysterious and exciting woman known as Holliday leads Brian into a life he never would have pictured for himself, a life of crime. The neurotic young man has to deal with a woman that's way out of his league, a childhood best friend turned police detective, and the heist of a lifetime, all while Brian does his best to not brown his trousers.

Brian and Holliday may have only just met, but if things don't go as planned then they might be spending the rest of their lives together, whether they want to or not.

www.ingramcontent.com/pod-product-compliance
Lightning Source LLC
Chambersburg PA
CBHW031959170626
46807CB00006B/2558